HARDCOVER HOMICIDE

ST. MARIN'S COZY MYSTERY - BOOK 9

ACF BOOKENS

1

The view outside the window of my bookstore, All Booked Up, was stunning. A light fog was just lifting from the street, and the rows of sugar maples that lined the sidewalks were brilliant in their gold/orange/red glory. Along their bases, their shed leaves were creating mosaics of color, and it looked like children had colored autumn all along our sidewalk.

It was my favorite season, and I was here for it – especially since my friend Rocky had whipped up the perfect pumpkin latte in the café she ran inside my shop. She didn't believe in artificial flavors for anything, so she and her mom had concocted a delicious syrup of pumpkin and vanilla that gave the drink its signature flavor and kept it from being the run-of-the-mill mixture that people bought in all the chain stores. I had to hold myself back from having more than one a day. It was so good.

It was a Tuesday morning, new release day, and while my assistant manager, Marcus, and I had gotten most of the displays ready after close last night, I was still at work early to fuss and ogle the new books. They made me so happy.

I was most excited, though, about the huge display we'd made in the window for Alix E. Harrow's newest book, *A Spindle Splintered*. I had become a huge fan of Harrow's work because of the way she wove fantasy and magic and the strength of women in her earlier books, and this novella was equally amazing with its retelling of the Cinderella myth with a twist of women's empowerment.

But the best part was that Harrow was coming to read from her new book here at my store on Saturday as part of her book tour. My friend Galen, an Instagram influencer of the best sort, had secured the attention of Harrow's publicist, and when he'd suggested my shop as a great venue, complete with a new reading area and stage, the date had been set. I'd been waiting two months for this, and I was fairly abuzz with excitement.

It was going to be the first event in my newly expanded store. My parents had generously financed the construction, and with my friends Walter and Woody in the lead, the project had been done in record time and even better than I could hope. The addition had let me expand my fiction section as well as add in a dedicated reading stage where I set up a display for the days when we didn't have events but that easily converted to a place for a podium or two arm chairs for a reading or conversation.

The guys had left the brick exposed around a huge plate-glass window just behind the stage, and my friend Elle, flower-grower extraordinaire, had put in a window box that took advantage of the west-facing sun and kept the space green and colorful all year long. The seating area in front of the stage was kept open with reading chairs when not in use, but my friends Cate and Mart and taken it upon themselves to collect old dining chairs so that we could have eclectic but comfortable seating for events.

Beyond the window, we had left a small alley between my shop and the hardware store next door, and in front of the addition, Walter had managed to create two parking spaces for those customers who wanted to run into either store without the trouble of parallel parking. The two brothers, Hugo and Horatio, who ran the store, were thrilled with all of the arrangement, and despite the fact that they lost several prime parking spaces for their shop, they'd been nothing but supportive.

In fact, beyond the plate glass window, they'd commissioned one of the artists from the art co-op that Cate ran in town to paint a book-themed mural of a little girl floating in a cloud with a book in hand. It was beautiful and so kind of them.

Now, though, I had to finish my opening chores, quit fiddling with Harrow's gorgeous book, and complete the final marketing items for the event on Saturday. Galen had volunteered to take on the ticket "sales" since we had limited space in the store and knew the demand would be high. He had managed to sell-out in two days, and now we were simply offering the last remaining seats to the people who came into our store and entered a drawing. Today was the day I would draw the names for the six remaining chairs, and I couldn't wait to call the winners.

But first, the store. I prepped the register and did one last walk-through to be sure everything looked tidy and cozy, and then I turned on the open sign, unlocked the door, and greeted my first customers, an older couple with silver hair and the most lovely walnut skin. They were looking for travel books about Iceland, and I escorted them to the travel section while asking about their trip.

"It's for our fiftieth wedding anniversary," she said. "The trip of a lifetime." She smiled at her husband, and he winked at her. I left them at the shelves and walked back to the register with a smile that only got wider when my phone dinged with a text from my boyfriend, Jared.

"Good Morning, Sunshine," it said. I could hear his voice in my head as I read the words, and I thought of him, in his police cruiser before he left for work, taking the time to write me.

"Good Morning, Moonshine," I replied.

The phone rang almost immediately. "I like that," he said. "And you know my affinity for the apple pie stuff."

I laughed. We'd thrown a potluck dinner at his house a couple weeks earlier, and Cate's husband, Lucas, had brought over some apple pie moonshine. It was so delicious and so high in proof that all of us were a little tipsy by the time our sausages had come off the grill, and Jared was a bit more "gone" than the rest of us. He'd had a little trouble serving the food without spilling it, in fact. "I do remember," I said. "I also remember your hangover the next day."

He groaned. "Don't remind me."

"Still on for lunch today?"

"Wouldn't miss it," he said. "See you then."

I put the phone down and watched the customers come in to browse or pick up one of Rocky's amazing drinks or pastries. Despite being two years into owning this store, sometimes it still felt like I was in some incredible dream, where everything I wanted in life has come true.

Today, though, that dream was interrupted when Taco, my Bassett Hound, decided to yak up the grass he'd eaten on the walk to work all over his raised dog bed on the stage. Fortunately, most of the customers were far enough away or weren't keyed into the gross sounds of a hound heaving, and so I was able to clean everything up without much attention. Taco, of course, had immediately gone back to sleep on Mayhem's dog bed before I even got the cleaning done, and now the two pups were snoring loudly side by side.

I gave the hounds some fresh water, placed a couple of treats near their water bowl for when they woke, and turned around to see my friends Walter and Stephen heading my way, large mugs of Rocky's delicious drinks in their hands. "Oh, hi! I didn't know you were coming in."

"Neither did we," Stephen said as he hugged me and then smiled at his husband. "We decided to come into town to get some flowers from Elle, and then everything looked so beautiful that we had to walk around. And of course, if we were going to walk anywhere, it was here."

Walter was looking over my shoulder at the stage and smiling.

"It really looks amazing," I said as I turned to stare with him. "Everything I hoped for and more. That planter box and the steps you all built around the edges of the stage so that it can also act as a reading amphitheater for kids – brilliant."

"That was all Woody's idea. He'd seen you crammed into the children's section with two dozen kids at your feet. He thought this might give you more space and bring in even more young customers," Walter said. "I think he's probably right."

"I know he is," I said as I glanced at my phone. "Storytime is in an hour, and I already have forty kids signed up."

Stephen laughed. "Want some help with wrangling?"

Walter shot Stephen a surprised look, and I laughed. These two men were decidedly and clearly childless by choice, so it was a bit out of character for Stephen to want to spend time with not just a couple children but a few dozen.

"What? You know I'm trying to get Harvey to bring me on as part of her marketing team. Got to get in good with the boss?" Stephen said with a wink at me.

"Oh," I said with genuine surprise. "Really? You want to work for me?"

Stephen blushed. "Well, yeah. I'm trying to get a small-business marketing agency started here. Had I not told you?"

I flashed back through our last conversations in my mind, and I honestly couldn't remember him having mentioned it.

"I'm sorry. So much has been going on, I must have forgotten." I scrunched up my face and said, "I'm a horrible friend."

"Oh, Stephen, let the woman off the hook," Walter said with a stern stare at his husband. "He's teasing you, Harvey. He is starting a business, but he only decided two days ago."

Stephen laughed. "Got you, though." He smiled. "I am interested in helping, though, Harvey, with both the kids and the marketing. *Pro bono* of course."

"I'd love the help, but I will pay you. This is your livelihood, and I believe in paying people for their work." I was adamant about that. Too many people, especially creative people, get asked to do their work for free, and I wasn't about to contribute to that culture of thinking creativity and art aren't real work. "Can you write up a proposal for me – mostly for my accountant – and then I can see what we can do?"

Stephen grinned. "Absolutely, but really, Harvey, don't feel any pressure. Your dad and I have talked a bit, and between his new business and mine, we think we might have a pretty good partnership there."

"Oh, I love that, too," I said. My dad had recently launched a consulting company to guide small businesses like mine as they decided whether or not to grow. He already had three clients, two of whom were local businesses, and I knew that once word got out he'd have clients from DC to Baltimore. "You'll make a great team."

"I think so, too," Walter said. "Now, what do we need to get ready for the horde of young people who will arrive."

As the three of us selected books – themed around fairytales to honor Harrow's reading – and prepped the coloring sheets I gave out after every story time, I thought about Stephen's new enterprise, Walter's growing contracting business, my friend Elle's expansion, which she was undertaking with Dad's guidance, and my own store. At a time when downtown communities were struggling but trying so hard to come back and be the center of their towns, our was well on its way. St. Marin's had never been short on tourist business in the summer, but now it looked like we might all thrive in the cooler months, too, which was a relief for all of us since it took off the pressure for those four months of warmth.

STORY TIME WENT off without a hitch, especially since Walter and Stephen seemed to have an unnoted penchant for using humor to wrangle children on their way to wild. And Stephen's monkey impersonation was actually very high-caliber.

As I rang up the numerous purchases that always came at the end of the hour, Marcus began straightening up the amphitheater. He'd come in as story time started and managed the rest of the store while I read, and I wondered, not for the first time, how I had even made it the first few weeks in the shop without him. He had proven himself to be an amazing manager, but he was, even more importantly in my eyes, an incredible bookseller. He read constantly, he knew how to talk about the aspects of a book that would interest different kinds of readers, and he was enthusiastic about books in a way that even I couldn't muster most days.

Now, as he picked up discarded juice boxes and stray coloring sheets, I heard him recommend *Change Sings* by Amanda Gorman. Wisely, he avoided noting that Gorman had spoken at President Biden's inauguration, just in case the young father wasn't a fan of our standing president, but he did point out that the rhythm of the words in the book was magical and full of imagery that he thought his young daughter, who stood nearby with the best fishtail braid I'd ever seen, would enjoy.

The man bought that book and two others from me, and when he left, I gave Marcus a big thumbs up. "Nice recommendation," I said.

"The little girl was humming 'Puff The Magic Dragon' the

whole time she was coloring. I thought it a likely fit." He bent down and retrieved a tiny car from beneath a table and tossed it to me for the lost and found. Someone would be in to get that sooner or later, I expected.

When Jared arrived a few minutes later, the store was bustling but tidy, and Marcus was all set to manage things while I stepped out for an hour. "Bring you anything I asked him?"

"Nope," he said. "Rocky brought me lunch today." The blush that rose up his cheeks was charming, but I knew the two of them were getting closer and closer as a couple. I expected that there might be a proposal in the works soon, but I was learning to mind my own business and not push. So I didn't ask.

"See you soon," I said as I took Jared's arm, let him scoop up the dog leashes, and headed out the door. Tuesday lunches had become a part of our dating routine, alongside Thursday night dinners at one of our houses each week. We were both people who appreciated a routine, and since I got almost as much pleasure out of anticipating something as I did doing it, the two dates I knew were coming always gave me a kick of joy each week.

"Where to?" I asked as we strolled toward the art co-op at the end of the street.

"Well, I thought maybe we'd do a walk through town just to get our appetites up all the way, and then Lu has promised me something special when we get back to her truck." Jared beamed at me. He loved giving surprises, and he knew I loved getting them.

"Perfect," I said and pulled his arm closer to me. "What's the surprise?"

He threw back his head and laughed. "You always ask that, and I never tell you. What do you think would make this time any different?"

I smiled. "Maybe you're growing weak under my constant interrogation."

Jared rolled his eyes. "I'm a police officer, Harvey. I'm trained to resist interrogation," he said in his best deep voice.

"You're not a spy, sir." I laughed.

"How do you know?"

"Touché."

We strolled along talking about our days and watching the dogs pick up every random scent deposited on the street in the last few hours. As we passed friends, we waved and stopped to chat, and so it was that we spent almost a half-hour walking before we got back to Lu's truck.

There, the surprise awaited – a full platter of chicken mole tacos with salsa verde, chips, and churros. "Violà," Lu said. "Just for you; our new special." She set two tangerine soda bottles on the counter and smiled.

"Oh, I love that you're adding platters. How cool!" I said as I grabbed the tray with gusto.

"Simpler for me and the customers, and easier to order for take-out, too," Lu said with a wink.

"I'll keep that in mind for Saturday," I said. Part of the arrangement for our author reading was that Harrow would come early for a casual dinner with staff and a few friends and have a chance to get to know some booksellers as well as relax. This kind of thing was something I was trying to build into my author events all the time. I wanted the author to feel connected to our community and my store, not just like they were part of some commodity we were selling.

"Excellent," Lu said. "Now enjoy your lunch." She smiled and moved to the customer behind us in line.

Jared led us over to the bench that sat just in front of my store. It was our usual Tuesday spot, and I loved it because it meant I got to watch people come and go from the shop without doing the work of greeting them.

I had just made my way through my first taco when a loud bang sounded behind me from the alley beside my store. Jared jumped up and ran over because, I expected, he thought the same thing I did: gun shot. But when I followed him to the alley, I was surprised to find that the scene was even more horrible.

A woman lay crumpled on the gravel, and beside her, a bright orange nail gun sat leaning against the wall of my store. Jared knelt down and then looked at me. "She's gone."

He had his phone out and to his ear before I could even think of what to do.

Just then, Hugo and Horatio came up the alley, presumably from their back door that opened onto it. "We heard something," Hugo said just before he dropped to his knees. "Dear God, it's Catherine."

2

Sheriff Tucker Mason came over as soon as I called. As he and Jared processed the scene, I walked with Hugo and Horatio to the bench by the street. They were both a little pale, and given that they knew the victim, apparently, it seemed like they might both be in a little shock.

"You guys okay?" I asked as I put my phone back in my pocket after texting Rocky to ask her to bring out a couple glasses of sweet tea, the brothers' favorite drink.

Both of them shook their heads, and I took a seat between them and took their hands. "You knew her?"

Horatio nodded. "She used to work for us when she was in high school, but we've known her since she was a little girl." Horatio's voice caught, and he put a hand over his face.

"She grew up in foster care after her parents struggled with addiction. One of her favorite things as a child was to come into the store after school and spend hours pulling on the reels of chains in the back. She loved the sound of them and the feel of the metal going through her fingers," Hugo added.

I took a deep breath and thought about how I loved the sensation of wind against the back of my neck, especially when

I was feeling overwhelmed. I suspected the feeling did something to calm my nervous system down, and I wondered if the same had been true for Catherine. It had to have been so traumatizing for her to go through all that as a little girl.

"Then, when she got older and wanted to work, we helped her foster parents get her a work permit and gave her a job. She was great with customers, and she knew the store as well as we did by the time she graduated." Hugo's voice was quiet. "When she went up north to apprentice with a carpenter, we were so proud of her."

I waited because, clearly, there was more to say here, but the men both looked so pained that I didn't want to press.

Eventually, Horatio said, "But last we heard, she had fallen victim to the same demons that had grabbed her parents." He swallowed hard. "We hadn't seen her in about five years."

"Six," Hugo corrected. "She came back just after her twenty-first birthday." He shook his head. "It was hard seeing her that way."

Over the years, I'd had friends struggle with addictions of various sorts, and it was never easy to be the person watching, especially if you were someone like me – and, it seemed, like Hugo and Horatio – who always wanted to help. Usually, I found I needed to create some distance between the person and myself so that I didn't get caught up in enabling their struggle. It was painful for all of us.

I squeezed both of the their hands. "I'm sure she knew you loved her."

Horatio sucked in a tight breath. "I hope so. I really hope so."

Jared and Tuck came over, and when they nodded, I stood up. The brothers needed to give their statements, as would I, which meant I needed to step away. I moved over by the door to the shop and thanked Rocky as she brought out the brothers' teas and delivered them.

"You okay?" she asked as she came back to the shop door.

"Yeah, just sad ," I said. "They're really torn up." I tilted my head toward Hugo and Horatio.

She sighed. "Man, those guys are so nice. I hate to see them upset." She squeezed my arm and opened the door.

"Tell Marcus I'll be in as soon as I can?"

She nodded and let the door swing shut behind her.

I busied myself by deadheading the marigolds in the planter boxes in front of my store and tried to focus on the fact that Tuck had always solved every murder he'd encountered in our small town, which was probably the only reason most people kept coming back to St. Marin's. A small town with this murder rate probably wouldn't still be this much of a tourist destination if people didn't feel confident in the police presence.

But despite Tuck's great work as sheriff, he did have his detractors, mostly hateful racists who didn't like the idea of a black man being the primary law enforcement officer in the town. The campaigns supporting his opponent, Bryan Dooley, were getting more and more hateful, and while no one said anything about Tuck's ethnicity directly, the appeals to "real" Americans were certainly true to the white nationalism that Dooley purported more quietly.

I had spent the last month working hard for Tuck's campaign. Stephen, Walter, and I did some canvassing, and Mart had convinced her bosses at the winery to donate sizably to Tuck's re-election fund. If the poll numbers were accurate, our efforts were working, and Tuck as pulling ahead. But we all knew these last three weeks before the election in early November were the crucial time.

And this murder could either make or break Tuck's re-election. I took a deep breath and turned my thoughts to what else I could do to help our sheriff get elected. I was just cooking up a meet and greet plan for next week when Jared touched my arm and startled me enough to make me jump.

"Oh," he said as he pulled me into a hug, "I'm sorry, Harvey. I thought you heard me coming."

I laughed against his chest. "I didn't, but that's my fault. I was lost in thought." I looked over to where Hugo and Horatio were again sitting with their tea. "They okay?"

Jared shook his head. "Not really, but they will be." He pointed inside. "Want to give your statement with a latte in hand?"

I smiled. "You know me too well, sir."

"And I only hope to get to know you better," he said with a wink that made my heart skip.

We made our way into the café, and I ordered two lattes before joining Tuck at a table away from other customers. I'd been through this routine enough times to know that Tuck was going to be in professional mode for my statement, and I didn't want anyone else overhearing what I had to say lest it compromise their investigation.

"So tell me what happened," Tuck said in his most police-like voice.

I nodded. "I was just sitting on the bench out there, when I heard a loud sound from the alley beside the shop. It sounded sort of like a gun shot, but not quite."

"Rifle or shot gun?" he asked as he made notes.

"Rifle," I said.

He nodded. "Okay. Then what?"

I told him about running over with Jared, finding the body, and then Horatio and Hugo coming up the alley from the back-door of their store.

"You saw them come out the back door?" he asked.

I paused, took a breath, and said, "No. I just assumed."

He nodded and made a note. "Anything else?"

"They told you they knew the victim," I asked.

"They did," he said.

"Okay, then that's all." I took a long sip of my latte as I Tuck finished taking notes and Jared came back toward the table, hopefully he could come back to boyfriend mode now that the police business was finished.

Fortunately, I didn't have to wait long. Tuck pocketed his notebook. Jared sat down, sighed, and then reached across the table to take my hand. "You okay?"

"I am. Are Horatio and Hugo okay?" I asked.

Jared shook his head. "I don't really know. They're pretty shaken up, or at least Hugo was. I'll know more after I talk to Tuck about his interview with Horatio."

I squeezed his fingers and resisted the urge to ask all the questions streaming through my head. He and Tuck had the investigation under control, and my curiosity would only make things more complicated. So I returned to my thoughts about Tuck's election.

"What do you think about doing a "Get to know the Sheriff" event here at the store next week?" I was having second thoughts because, well, everyone in town pretty much knew Tuck if they wanted to, so maybe the idea was silly.

Jared grinned. "I love that idea. Maybe we could call it, Sheriff Share or something and let people know they can come and share their concerns with the sheriff."

"Ooh, I like that," I said. "More about showing how open he is to community feedback and less about sharing who he is."

"Exactly," Jared said as he moved his leg against mine under the table. "You're worried about the election?"

"Aren't you?" I asked.

He sighed. "I wish I wasn't because, honestly, does anyone actually think Bryan Dooley can do a better job than Tuck?"

"Of course not. They just think he's whiter than Tuck," I said a little too loudly. A couple of customers turned to look at me, but when they smiled, I remembered I was among friends here in my store. No one who shopped at a bookstore where two-thirds of the staff members were black would be willing to listen to Dooley's racist nonsense.

"And that's the scariest part, right? It would be awful for Tuck to lose, of course, but imagine a white nationalist as sheriff." He shivered.

I forced the lump of fear down in my throat and said, "Terrifying" just as I saw Tuck come back through the shop door. "Here comes Tuck," I whispered.

Jared gave me a wink and pulled his leg but not his hand back.

"Hey Tuck," I said. "Want a latte?"

"That would be great, but could I get two shots of espresso?" he asked as he stretched his arms above his head. "It may be a long day."

"Coming up," I said as I stood and headed back to the counter with the sheriff's order.

While Rocky made Tuck's drink, I scooted over to the shop to find Marcus and tell him about the event with the sheriff next week. He was at the register, checking inventory, so I gave him the low-down and asked if he could let Galen know.

"Definitely, and I'll make a poster, too, maybe change up the window display to a local history thing with Tuck's poster featured since he's a hometown boy." Marcus smiled.

"Great idea . . . ." Dooley was from Annapolis, and while the city was only an hour away, for most folks here on the Eastern Shore of Maryland, it might as well have been in California for how different the culture was. Here, people were rural or small-town proud, and we loved our watermen and water culture. Annapolis was where most of us went for fancy dinners or big shopping trips, but the Eastern Shore was home. "People will love that, and it'll give us a chance to feature some local authors, too. Might be a good draw for Harrow's event as well."

Marcus nodded. "I was going to redo the other window for

her reading, too. Cate made me a papier-mâché witch hat for the center. Okay with you?"

"Of course. I love that. Tell Galen about that, too, so he can get some pictures?" I asked.

"Definitely. Everything okay?" He glanced toward the two police officers in the café.

"Yes and no," I said and told him about Catherine and her relationship with Horatio and Hugo. "I'm sure they're suspects."

"Probably, but we know them. They're good guys. Tuck and Jared know that, too." Marcus patted my shoulder and turned to ring up a customer as I returned to the café, got Tuck's latte, and told him about where he would be next Tuesday night to help his election.

THE REST of the day went swimmingly. Marcus's window displays looked amazing, and between those and Galen's photos on Instagram, we already had queries about Tuck's event and more calls than I could count to see if we had any remaining tickets for Harrow's reading. After Dad came by and assured me that we could get two more seats into the reading area safely, I asked Galen to put out the word that I'd be drawing names for the final two seats at ten a.m. on Saturday morning.

The catch was that people had to come to the store to enter by dropping their names and numbers in the cauldron (a stock pot that I hurriedly painted black) in the window display. Entries would be open until eight p.m. on Friday night.

Folks started coming in right away to enter, and while some just popped in, filled out the entry slip, and left, many shopped, got coffee, or just hung out for a while. Tuesdays were usually quite busy, but this little marketing tactic has us really hopping. So much so, that when it was time for me to leave at five p.m., I offered to stay on and help Marcus close up.

"Woman, go home," he said with a laugh. "We have got this." He swung an arm toward Rocky and her assistant, Cecilia, in the café. "You open tomorrow, and you now have two massive events coming."

"Alright, I'm going." I was a bit sad to leave because I loved busy days in the shop. But tonight was silly TV night with Mart, and I couldn't wait to binge some more *Married at First Sight*. Cate had been raving about this show for months, and Mart and I had finally caved and started to watch. Now, we were as addicted as Cate was.

On the walk to our house, I let Mayhem and Taco lead the way. Sometimes they were eager to get home and eat, but on some days, like this crisp October evening, they meandered their way along scent trails that I was happy to follow, too. We walked through crunching leaves, and I marveled at the massive mums some of my neighbors had in their yards.

In my autumn-inspired stupor after a long day, I totally lost track of where we were walking until we doubled back along the long alley behind my shop. There, I was quickly dragged back to attention, though, when both Mayhem and Taco began tugging me hard down that direction. When they turned into the alley between the hardware store and my shop, I tried to slow them down because I wasn't sure that the alley had been opened after the murder this morning. But they were on a mission.

A mission that came sliding to a halt about two feet into the alley when both of them stopped and began sniffing in a shadowy space next to the hardware store wall. I pulled out of my phone and turned on the flashlight. I'd never seen a rat or a snake in this alley way, but I wasn't taking any chance that this would be the first time.

It wasn't a live critter that my pups were smelling though. It was a glove, one of those blue ones that doctors or immune-suppressed people used to keep from getting sick. I looked around to see if maybe someone had dropped the other, but this seemed to be the only one. And my dogs wouldn't leave it alone. Something was up.

I pulled the dogs the rest of the way up the alley, as I alternated apologizing for the tugging on their necks and berating them for being obstinate until I reached the parking area by the front of my store. There, I stopped, noticed the police tape was gone, and called Jared.

"The dogs found something in the alley. Can you come?"

"On my way," he said, and a few minutes later, he jogged up from the direction of his house. He was wearing a flannel shirt and jeans, and he looked amazing in his slightly mussed state. "What did they find?"

"You guys searched this alley, right?" I asked as I led him back to the glove.

"We did, but we didn't find anything." He stopped, though, as I shone my light on the glove. "That wasn't there before."

"The dogs are certainly interested," I said as I looked back at where I had tied them to the bench in front of the shop to keep them disturbing the glove. I could see them straining to get back to us. "They led me right here."

Jared took out a pair of his own gloves and picked up the one from the ground. "Do you have a bag in the shop that I can use? I didn't exactly come prepared."

I nodded. "Sure thing." We walked back into the shop, and when Marcus raised an eyebrow, I said, "Just here for a bag."

As Marcus reached for one, Jared said, "Let me" and used his gloved hands to pull one off the stack below the register before dropping the glove from the alley into the bag. "Thanks."

Marcus eyed the back. "Evidence?"

"Maybe," Jared said. "But you saw nothing."

"That is not the glove you are looking for," Marcus droned as he winked at me. "Now, go home, Harvey."

"On my way," I said as Jared and I went back out front.

"I'd offer to talk you home," Jared said, "but—"

"But you need to get that to the station. Want some company on the walk?" I asked as I untied the dogs.

"Always," he said and headed toward the station with the dogs, again, leading the way. "I expect this is just something someone dropped, but it's good to check."

"Yeah, I figured. And given that the dogs were so interested . . ." I looked at my two pups who were sniffing and walking steadily ahead, unlike their behavior in the alley.

"Exactly." He stopped in front of the station. "Be right back." He smiled at me and went inside.

A couple moments later he was back out and extending his arm to me. "Now, I can walk you home, if that's okay with you," he said.

"Of course. But I'll warn you that if you stay around, you will be forced to watch a reality show where people get married without having met." I braced myself for his reaction.

"Well, as fascinating as that sounds, I was right in the middle of sanding some drywall, so I won't be able to stay." He laughed.

"Oof, you know it's bad when sanding drywall sounds better than watching TV with your girlfriend." I winked at him.

"Nothing ever sounds better than spending time with you, but I also want to finish this project, want to give you and Mart your time, and really do *not* want to watch that show." He pulled me into his side as we walked.

"Three solid reasons," I said. "Besides, we're having salad for dinner." My boyfriend ate very healthily, and he loved a good salad, but only if it was covered in meat, dressing, and cheese.

"I expect there won't be any bleu cheese dressing, right?" he said with a chuckle.

"Nope, or if there is, it'll be in a bowl so you have to dip your fork in to get any." The first time I'd done this fork-dipping technique when we'd had dinner out, Jared had laughed at me because he said the point of the salad was the dressing.

When I'd argued that the point of the salad was the cucumbers, he'd rolled his eyes and then rolled them even harder when I said the lettuce also mattered. Now, it was a standing joke between us – the pourer, him, and the dipper, me.

"I'll pass on dinner then," he said as he gave me a quick kiss at my front door. "Have fun."

"Oh, we will." I smiled as I opened the door and stepped inside. "Enjoy the drywall."

"Oh, I will," he said and waved as he jogged up the street. Goodness, he looked good.

Inside, Mart was well on her way to making an amazing salad complete with just a little cheese, homemade croutons, honey mustard dressing (on the side), and hardboiled eggs. We had both taken a month off of bacon because it was becoming a bit of addiction in our house, so I would miss that addition. But still, this looked amazing.

I took the glass of white wine she handed me and picked up my salad bowl with the little cup of dressing inside it. "Picnic?" I asked.

"You read my mind," she said as she grabbed her own bowl and followed me and the dogs outside.

Our backyard was slowly but surely becoming a real refuge. We'd landscaped with some foundational shrubs, as Jared's mom called them, and we'd decided to plant a Japanese maple beside the patio to give shade and color. Just now, the red leaves were dancing in the evening breeze, and it was gorgeous.

A small glass-top table and two chairs sat on the patio. We placed our glasses and bowls there next to a small candle Mart had lit for us. It was a cool night, and I went back inside to grab a sweater for me and a hoodie for Mart. Then, we ate as Mart filled me in about her day at the winery which had included a surprise visit from Dwayne "The Rock" Johnson.

"He is quite the wine expert," she said, "and you know what his favorite varietal is?"

Mart was clearly excited to share this information despite my still-lacking knowledge of exactly what a varietal was, so I nodded.

"Sangiovese." She smiled. "That's fitting given how robust he is."

"That's one word for it," I said with a laugh. "Have you told Symeon you spent the day with a movie star?"

"Told him. I texted him as soon as I knew the man was coming. Symeon came right over and used our new pizza oven to make The Rock lunch." She chewed another forkful of salad. "I think Symeon has a bigger crush on him that I do."

"And how did the pizza go over?" I asked after finishing my own bite of salad.

Mart leaned forward. "So well that he's invited Symeon to help him build one at his farm in central Virginia." Her eyes were gleaming.

"And I take it you will get to go along on this trip?" I laughed.

"Of course. I'll be evaluating his land to see if its suitable for grape cultivation, of course," she flipped her long dark hair over her shoulder and grinned.

"Any need for a bookstore consultant or a police officer's presence on this trip?" I asked without even trying to mask my jealousy.

"Actually, no, but I did ask if we could bring two friends, and Dwayne – he asked me to call him Dwayne – said of course. So we are going next weekend." Mart stared at me as I let my mouth fall open.

"Are you serious?" I said.

"Totally. It's peak color season out there, Dwayne said, so

we'll go out, tour the property on Friday, do the oven build on Saturday, and enjoy a relaxing Sunday before heading back." She put her hand on mine. "And before you come up with some excuse about the store, I already talked to Marcus. He's got it covered, and Tuck gave Jared the weekend off, too. So you have no reason not to go."

I hadn't really been thinking about reasons not to go. This sounded like too much of a good thing to pass up, especially after a busy week. But I did appreciate that Mart had already figured out logistics before telling me. If Jared or Marcus had balked, I would have felt a little guilty about going, but I probably still would have gone. This way, we can all enjoy guilt-free.

I needed to have a little fun with Mart, though, so I said, "What about Symeon? Surely, Max can't spare him for an entire weekend?" I kept my face as serious as I could.

Mart rolled her eyes. "You are the worst liar, Harvey Beckett. That's already taken care of, too. The new sous-chef has it covered, and given that Symeon is doing this build as an employee of Chez Cuisine, Max gets a cut, too. They're actually thinking of creating another income stream if this venture works out. Max was very excited."

I grinned. "Well, then I suppose you have managed all my objections," I said as I cut my eyes at her, "as if I really had any to begin with." I plunged into my salad as I tried to keep my mind focused on our weekend away in just nine days, but my brain kept steering me back to Catherine's murder and that glove.

Apparently, I was lost in thought longer than I realized because Mart put her hand on my fork as it began its climb to my mouth again and said, "Okay, what's up with you?"

I looked down and saw that I had eaten almost my entire meal without noticing any of it. So much for all the work on mindfulness I'd been doing lately. I sighed, put down my fork, and said, "I found a dead body today."

A year ago, Mart might have been shocked or worried when I told her such news, but today she simply said, "Of course you did," and took another bite of chicken. After she chewed and swallowed, she said, "Okay, tell me about it."

I sighed and filled her in on the days' events, all the way to the dogs finding the glove. "Jared is sure the glove wasn't there earlier, though, so that's weird."

Mart nodded. "That is odd given that it was a glove, I guess, but people litter back that way all the time, Harvey. Someone probably just dropped it."

"Maybe." I looked over to where Taco and Mayhem were digging a trench through the yard in hot pursuit of a vole and said, "but then why were the dogs so interested in it?"

"Fried chicken is my guess. Someone was using the glove to keep their hands clean while they ate fried chicken." Mart looked at me intently. "Don't go looking for mysteries where there aren't any, Harvey. You have enough on your plate."

I knew she was probably right, but something about that glove was irking me. I couldn't get a handle on what, though, so I said, "Okay, so let me tell you about my plan to help Tuck's re-election."

"Not without dessert," Mart said and produced a pastry bag with two chocolate croissants. "We need sustenance for all your plans."

3

Fortunately for my sleep routine, Mart and I got so annoyed with one of the new husbands on our show that we made it an early night, and I was sound asleep by ten. Unfortunately at two a.m., Aslan, my queen of a cat, decided it was time to share my pillow but only after it was fluffed to her exact specifications.

So I was awake for a bit right in the middle of the night because my brain kicked in as soon as my eyes opened. Fortunately, I had begun to be a lot better about controlling my thoughts and forced myself to think about what Mart and I were going to plant next in our new native flower bed beside the house instead of spiraling into my list of to-dos and worries for the week.

When my alarm went off at six-thirty, Aslan was pressed against the back of my skull, and she was snoring. I've said it before, and I'll say it again: it's a good thing animals are cute. I slid myself out of bed carefully, so as not to disturb Her Highness, and headed for a shower and then coffee.

I'd started getting up early so that I could actually enjoy my morning instead of feeling like I was just rushing off to work.

My ritual began, as most of my rituals did, with coffee, and then I lit a candle and sat down in my reading chair with my latest book, *The Library of the Dead* by T. L. Huchu. The book was fantasy and ghosts and post-apocalyptic desperation in the best way, and I savored the time I gave myself to read a few chapters each morning.

Then with words in my brain, I put some food into my belly. This morning, I made an egg white, spinach, and cheese omelette and enjoyed it while I watched the dogs sniff around on their morning constitutional in the backyard. The way they wandered told me exactly where the squirrels had been on their nocturnal ventures, and I couldn't help but think about how very intently the dogs had sniffed that glove.

Sure, it could have been fried chicken or cheese or chocolate or anything edible really, but sadly, I'd had enough experience with murders in the past couple of years that I thought there was more to it than that.

Sadly, I wasn't wrong, as I learned when Jared texted me on our walk to the store. "Blood on the glove. Probably Catherine's. See you at the shop?"

"Be there in ten," I said and picked up the pace a bit. I wasn't one to say, "I told you so," but Mart had been way off about this one.

When I arrived, Jared was waiting at the door, and he didn't look happy. "Good morning," I said as I gave him a hug and a kiss on the cheek. "Long morning already?"

He nodded. "Any chance I can get a coffee while we talk?" His face was pale, and the circles under his eyes spoke volumes.

"Absolutely. Rocky is usually in by now, and if she's not, I'll make an espresso for your myself." I took his arm and led him inside before locking the door behind me.

My lattes aren't bad at all, but Rocky is, by far, the best barista I've ever met. I don't know if it's how long she steams the milk, the way she grinds the espresso, or just some magic she slips into the brew, but her hot drinks are far above and beyond anything I've ever had in my life, except for maybe the ones this coffee shop owner in the Outer Richmond used to make for me in San Francisco. I think he and Rocky are tied.

So this morning, Jared lucked out, and Rocky made him a stellar espresso with just a hint of cinnamon and vanilla to give him a little boost for the day. We waited quietly at the counter while she worked, and even though I was dying to know what had been found on the glove, it seemed wise, given Jared's silence, to let him manage the conversation.

When we sat down with our drinks, he told me the whole deal. Apparently, there was not just blood on the glove but blood splatter.

"Like from a wound? Could you tell the direction of the injury?" I blurted before thinking about what I was saying.

Fortunately Jared's reaction was mirth and not disdain. He threw his head back and laughed. "Alright, Crime Scene Tech Beckett, what do you hope we could ascertain from a balled up glove left in the back of an alley?"

I knew when I was being mocked, but given Jared's levity, I decided to roll with it. "Were there fibers? Hairs maybe? Epithelial tissue?"

Jared's smile grew wide. "Yes, yes, and yes."

"What?! OH, that's great news. Solving the case should be so easy then." I was going way beyond in my exaggeration here, but my boyfriend needed a good laugh. And at least a small part of me hoped I wasn't exaggerating.

He leaned over and kissed me. "Thank you, Harvey. I needed that."

"Needed what?" I said with wide eyes. "You can't solve the case with your microscope and mass spectrometer."

He laughed again. "When our town budget affords us a mass spectrometer or even a microscope for that matter, I'll let you know." He kissed my fingers. "The fibers, hair, and tissue were all residue from the alley, we think, since they were on the outside of the glove."

I paused a minute. "How did you find all that without even a microscope?" I said. This time I was serious.

"We Sherlock a bit." Jared held up his hand and pretended to pull a magnifying glass to his face. "It's old school but effective."

This time, I laughed out loud. "Fair enough. But the blood is Catherine's?"

He nodded. "The type is right. That's all we can test for here, but I expect it'll be a match when we get it back from the lab. Tuck asked them to rush it."

I sat back and stared across the store, which was, of course, immaculate since Marcus had closed the night before. "Why would the glove show up later, though? That seems so weird."

"It is odd, but it's also possible we missed it in our initial search." Jared got a little crease between his eyebrows when he was puzzled, and it was very deep at the moment.

"I guess," I said, "but maybe it showed up later. Like could the killer have come back to see the scene of the crime." I knew I was stretching here, but I also knew that was, in fact, something that intense killers did.

"Maybe," Jared nodded. "But usually those folks show up while the police are there. They like to feel like they're pulling one over on the authorities."

I smiled. "I think I remember Reid saying something like that on *Criminal Minds*," I joked.

"Of course, he said it verbatim from some book he studied, right?" Jared teased me about my love of crime shows, but he was just as much of an avid viewer as I was.

"Of course, and he mooned over J. J. while he said it." I leaned over and kissed Jared's cheek as I stood up. "You'll keep me posted . . . I mean as it's appropriate to do so?"

Jared stood and hugged me close. "Of course, as appropriate." He walked me to the register in the bookstore. "I was actually wondering if we could maybe do one of those in-store potlucks tonight. Not to talk about the case but maybe just to get together with friends."

I looked at his face for a long moment and said, "Of course. I'll put the word out to everyone." Jared had never asked to get together with my friends – now our friends – before, but I definitely understood the need for companionship and distraction on a hard day. "See you here at seven?"

"I wouldn't miss it," he said and gave me another quick kiss. "Have a great day."

I followed him to the door and locked it behind him. I had fifteen minutes to prep for the day, and I would need every minute to get the register ready and my second latte at the counter.

THE DAY BEGAN with an enthusiastic crowd ready to shop, get hot coffee, and enter the drawing for tickets to Harrow's reading. I estimated we already had fifty entries, and we still had three more days before the drawing. It was exciting.

I helped a woman in her sixties find some books on knitting from the newly expanded craft section, and she oohed and awed for Lori Rea's book on needle felting. "I can make all my grandkids' Hanukkah presents," she said.

Between her joy and my caffeinated system, I was fairly buzzing by the time Marcus came in at eleven. He was thrilled to hear about the potluck and decided he'd try his hand at crockpot beef stew in the back room. "Give me thirty, and I'll have this place smelling heavenly," he said as he dashed out to the grocery store just up the road.

I wasn't sure beef stew was the scent most bookstore shoppers savored for their experience, but I couldn't squash his enthusiasm . . . and I, for one, loved the scent of beef stew. I texted Mom to ask if she could make some of her famous beer bread to go with it, and she replied with an enthusiastic two thumbs up. She was just getting the hang of emojis, and it was a delight to watch her answer every possible message with some cute image.

Everyone else replied just as enthusiastically, but with fewer emojis, to my text about the potluck, and soon we had a whole array of delicious foods planned. When Stephen and Walter suggested they bring their new fall cocktail to share, I was more certain than ever that tonight was going to be fun. I hoped Jared could find some laughter in the evening, too.

THE AFTERNOON WHIZZED by as people came in to enter the Harrow reading contest and then browsed a bit. I was glad I'd ordered more copies than I had originally intended of her work because they were flying off the shelves before she even arrived in town.

My favorite customer of the day was a man who looked to be about forty, spoke with a South African accent, and wanted the best spy novel I could recommend. He was already a fan of Vince Flynn, so I recommended Stephen Leather's Spider Shepherd series. He picked up the first three, bought them, and then took a seat in the café after telling me he took one afternoon a month off from work just to read. That was the best reading plan I'd ever heard, especially from a professional man in midlife, and I hoped we might see him in here more often to get his spy-thriller fix.

By mid-afternoon, the store was fairly redolent with the aroma of cooking stew, and several customers asked Rocky if she was selling soups now. She said she wasn't, but when she came over to ask me if I thought soups might sell, I wasn't surprised. This woman was an entrepreneur at heart.

"Maybe start with Marcus's beef stew," I said with a wink.

"Definitely," she said, "and I can make an incredible potato leek for Friday."

I was already savoring the idea of soup for lunch most days when an older man with a shock of white hair, thick glasses, and a pasty pallor came into the store. I noted him especially because he seemed unwell, like he was nauseated or something. He kept stopping against the tables to catch his breath and then wiping his brow.

"Would you like to sit down?" I said as I approached him.

He nodded, and I led him to the closest chair in the history section and then told him I'd be back with a glass of water.

When I returned, a bit of color had returned to his face, and as he sipped the cold drink, a pink flush rose up in his pale cheeks. "Feeling better?" I asked.

"Thank you," he said as he raised the glass to me. "It's been quite a day." He took another sip and then watched as I slid a chair over to him.

"Bad news?" I asked, not wanting to be nosy but also knowing that sometimes the thing I most wanted was for someone to notice I needed to talk.

"The worst," he said. "My daughter was killed yesterday."

I swallowed hard. Catherine's father. "I'm so sorry."

He finished off the water and handed the glass back to me. "I thought coming back to town would help, might help me feel closer to her again. But then I saw the place—" he threw a hand to his mouth and stifled a sob.

I put my hand on his arm. His grief was intense, and unfortunately, I'd learned from experience that no words really helped someone suffering like this. So I just sat and let him cry.

After a few minutes, he took a few deep breaths and looked up at me. "I'm sorry," he whispered.

"Sorry for what? Caring about your daughter? Please, never apologize for that, and tears are no reason for apology either." I sat back as he wiped his face and did the same. "Tell me about her?"

A small smile lifted the corner of his lips as he gazed back into the bookstore behind me. "She was an amazing kid. So smart and funny, but she didn't take flak from anyone. Learned that before she came to live with us, I guess." His smile faded.

I had a lot of questions, but for many reasons, I just stayed quiet and let him talk.

"Once when she was four, a little girl at school was mean to her, so Catherine head-butted her. It took her mother everything we had not to laugh when we knew we needed to give her some options beyond physical violence." He glanced up at me.

"I totally get it. Good for her for defending herself," I said.

His smile grew wide. "She never was one to back down, never. She challenged her mother and me every step of the way, but she was worth it, even as a teenager when we really, really wondered if we'd all make it."

I smiled. I didn't have children, but I always appreciated candor when others talked about their children. It felt like they were honoring the fullness of the child's humanity instead of making them specimens to be adored.

"But then she turned eighteen, and she got this idea in her head that she needed to be on her own. Needed to figure out how to take care of herself." He shook his head. "We told her she could stay with us as long as she wanted, even though she was out of the system by then. She was our daughter. But her first few years had been too brutal for her to trust that, I guess."

"She was in the foster system?" I asked, even though I already knew the answer.

He nodded. "She was. We got her when she was three and a half and just a ball of anxiety and attitude. But we loved her from the start and were able to keep her with us for almost fifteen years."

"That's wonderful," I said and thought about all the stories

I'd read about children in foster care who get moved from house to house or have traumatic experiences in their foster homes. It sounded like Catherine had gotten an amazing place to grow up.

"For all of us. She is—," he cleared his throat, "she *was* our light." Tears welled in his eyes again as he looked at me.

"I am so sorry for your loss, and thank you for telling me about Catherine." I sighed and knew it was probably better to be up front with him. "Sir – I'm sorry, I didn't catch your name. I'm Harvey Beckett."

"Roger Birmingham," he said and put out his hand to shake mine, a reflexive action if ever I saw one.

I shook his hand and then held onto it with both of mine. "I am the one who found your daughter yesterday. I'm so terribly sorry."

He crushed my fingers between his. "You are? Did you see who did this to her? Was it one of those brothers who were always paying way too much attention to her?"

I tilted my head. "Horatio and Hugo from the hardware store? They paid too much attention to your daughter?" I didn't know the brothers too well, but they both struck me as very kind people. Maybe a little odd but always kind and generous.

Mr. Birmingham shook his head and frowned. "I'm sorry. I'm probably not thinking straight. I shouldn't have said that." He sighed. "How did Catherine look?"

I paused and thought about what he really wanted to know. After all, she'd been murdered with a nail gun, so I didn't think he was asking for a literal description. I pictured her face and said, "She looked peaceful."

He let out a shuddering breath. "Good. She deserved peace." He stood up then and looked down at me. "Thank you, Ms. Beckett."

"Please call me Harvey, and if you need anything you can find me here or someone will know where I am." I stood and walked him to the door. "Have you talked to the police yet? I'm sure they would want to learn more about Catherine, too."

He nodded. "Yeah, I'm going there now. The station is just up the street, right?"

"Yep, just up the way. And Mr. Birmingham, Tucker Mason, our sheriff, and Jared Watson are good men. Jared is my boyfriend, in fact. They're already working hard to figure out what happened to Catherine, I assure you." I reached over and hugged him.

He patted my back and said, "Thank you again" before walking out to the street.

I turned my back to the window, took out my phone, and called Jared. He answered on the first ring. "Catherine's father, Roger Birmingham, is on his way to see you. He was just here."

Jared groaned quietly. "Okay. Thanks for the heads up. How is he?"

"Very kind, but he did say something about suspecting that Horatio or Hugo had something to do with her death. Just an FYI."

I could almost feel Jared sighing up the street. "Okay, then. See you soon?"

"I'll be here with a hug." He sounded so exhausted.

"I'll need it." He hung up, and I stood in the middle of the store for a minute as all the weight of this situation settled a bit more onto my shoulders.

As soon as I ushered the last customer, a charming man with a waxed moustache and a fedora who was very invested in books on dahlias, out of the door and turned off the open sign, a steady stream of my friends arrived bearing all kinds of food, including a salad with apples and walnuts that looked amazing. Combine that with Marcus's stew, Mom's beer bread, and the lemon bars that Lucas had just added to his cupcake menu, and I was going to be eating well tonight.

Stephen and Walter's cocktail, a bourbon pumpkin splash, was delicious and gave my belly just the right amount of warmth after a couple of chilling days. Being the men that they were, they had also printed out copies of the recipe from a woman named Meghan at the Cake and Knife blog and handed them out to anyone who wanted to create this deliciousness. I took one for sure.

Jared arrived just a few minutes after seven, and he looked even more haggard than earlier. I had a drink ready for him and put it in his hands as soon as I reached him. Then, I pulled him behind a bookshelf and gave him a slow kiss and long hug.

When I pulled back, he shook his head and smiled. "Well, thank you," he whispered against my neck as he tugged me close again. "I needed that."

"I thought so," I said. "You okay?"

"I am. Just very tired, and Birmingham's visit wasn't easy, especially at the end of a long day."

I stared at him for a second. "Is this something you want to talk about now, later, or never?"

"How about later?" he said as he smiled at me. "Now, I'd like to eat. Whatever that scent is, it's making my stomach growl."

"You got it." We headed back to the reading area where our friends had already begun to fill bowls and plates with food. Marcus's beef stew looked amazing with its bright orange carrots and yellow potato wedges. I couldn't wait to taste it.

I filled my plate and my bowl and made my way to the floor next to the chair where Jared was sitting. I scooted myself right against his leg, not sure if I was trying to comfort him or find comfort for myself, and tucked into the food. The stew was amazing, and with Mom's bread, I felt like I had just settled into a rustic cabin in the woods with a fire blazing.

We had, in fact, considered putting a fire place in when we

did the addition to the store, but the fire chief had suggested that loose sparks, even from a propane stove, might not be the best idea in a building full of paper. And since I really wanted a wood-burning fireplace anyway – I loved the scent – we forewent the entire plan. Later, it turned out that it had been a good idea for more reasons than just a fire hazard since I learned that people with asthma sometimes really struggled in rooms with wood-burning fires.

Now, though, I thought about creating a paper one on the wall just for the effect and decided that would be my next project, after Harrow's reading and Tuck's meet and greet. Right now, I had enough going on without trying to be crafty.

The conversation moved lightly around the room as Lucas updated us on the latest pirate exhibition at the maritime museum. He'd timed the display to coincide with Halloween, but besides the kitschy black and white striped pirates in the museum, the display was much more about the hellions that pirates had actually been. As Lucas said, "Blackbeard wasn't exactly the kind of guy you want to revere."

Henri, our friend who was a weaver with a studio at Cate's art co-op, shared about her latest commission for a local celebrity who wanted a water-themed hanging created to place over the grand staircase in her foyer. "twenty feet by thirty feet," Henri said. "I've never made anything that big, but I can't wait to try."

"Are you using all blues and grays?" Elle asked between mouthfuls of her own delicious salad. "Or are you doing your signature bright colors?"

Henri smiled. "Both. The water will be the background in blues, grays, and greens, and then I'm doing a couple of small fishing ships in a sort of quilt-like pattern. I'm hoping the client likes it, but since she already paid me and gave me directions to be creative, I get to do what I want. It's exciting."

I looked at my friend and studied the way joy showed

against her walnut complexion. She fairly glowed when she talked about her work, and I loved that. I hoped I looked the same when I talked about books.

We got updates on Bear's work at the hospital and Pickle's wild but anonymous stories about his legal clients. And everyone talked about how excited they were that Alix Harrow was coming this weekend. I had basically forced everyone to read *The Ten Thousand Doors of January* by buying them all copies, telling them it was my new favorite book, and then having the central occupation of the story, "wordworker," tattooed on my arm.

To their credit, every one of these people had read the book and while they hadn't all permanently inked themselves with a memory of it, they had all appreciated the storytelling. Cate had even gone so far as to do a series of photographs of artistic doors, including an installation of a door in a field like the central one in the book, to display this weekend. I couldn't wait to show it to Harrow when she arrived on Saturday afternoon.

Tuck and Lu had been remarkably quiet as they ate their dinner, and their expressions read as preoccupied and even worried. Eventually, Mart couldn't take it any longer and said, "Masons, why the long faces?"

Symeon looked at her and grinned. "That almost rhymed."

"I'm a poet, and I didn't—" Mart began before I groaned and interrupted her.

"Yeah, are you okay?" I looked at my two friends.

Lu glanced at Tuck and said, "My husband doesn't want me to say anything, but you are our closest friends. We need you. Tuck received a threat today."

I felt Jared stiffen against my leg and looked up at him. His eyes were wide, but I couldn't tell if he was surprised by the news or surprised because Lu shared it.

"A threat?" Pickle said, leaning forward from his leather wingback chair. "What kind of threat?"

"A death threat," Tuck said with a sigh. "The note was left on the door of the station and said that if I didn't pull out of the election, I wouldn't have any more breath to waste on campaigning anyway."

A hiss of shock spun through the room. "Do you know who sent it?" Elle asked.

Tuck met her eyes and said, "I have no proof of who sent it."

The careful wording of that statement didn't get past me, and I expected our friends noted it, too. But we knew better than to press Tuck on an investigation, especially one this sensitive.

"What are you going to do?" I asked quietly.

Tuck looked at me and rolled his eyes. "I'm quitting, Harvey. I'm going to retire and read novels all day. Got any recommendations?"

I smiled. "Now that you mention it . . ." I sighed. "But really?" All of us knew that Tuck loved his job, would never go down without a fight, and certainly wasn't going to cower at a threat.

Jared shifted next to me. "I'm taking the lead on that investigation. We're going to find proof of who did this and take appropriate action." His words were formal, but I could hear the barely withheld emotion behind the words. He was livid.

I put my hand around his calf and squeezed. No wonder he was exhausted. This was a lot for anyone, but given the personal nature of the threat against Tuck. "I have no doubt," I said to him, and everyone around the room nodded.

"Now, who is up for some lemon bars?" Tuck asked as he stood and made his way back to the table.

After some of us exchanged glances of concern, we stood and moved behind Tuck to scoop up Lucas's delicious treats and let Tuck change the subject. None of us were going to leave the search for the person who threatened our friend go, though, not even if lemon bars were involved.

4

After we all cleaned up for dinner and headed out, Symeon and Jared walked Mart and me home. While the dogs sniffed and snuffled their way through the early evening, we huddled together in the cooling night as much for comfort as for warmth, I think.

About halfway to our house, Mart said, "We all know this is Bryan Dooley, right?"

Jared looked at her out of the corner of his eye but didn't say anything.

I, however, had no ethical quandary here so I said, "Darn right it is! The nerve." Next to me, Jared stifled a giggle, and I smiled.

"So let's pretend we don't know any police officers or that they suddenly have put on noise cancelling headphones while they listen to Nirvana as we walk, okay?" Symeon said with a wry smile.

Jared started humming "Come As You Are," took Mayhem and Taco's leashes, pulled away to walk a few steps ahead of us. Man, he was a good sport.

"What do you have in mind, sir?" Mart asked as she pulled him closer to her.

"There is no way that Dooley will believe either of you is interested in his campaign, but he doesn't know me except as a chef. What if I went undercover in his campaign?" Symeon's eyes were wide with excitement.

"You think that will work?" Mart asked. "I mean, doesn't he know we're dating?"

"He might, but I could play that off as need be. People have different politics and all that," Symeon said.

I had lots of hesitations, and by the way Jared's footfalls were slowing and letting him get closer and closer to us, I gathered he did, too. But I wasn't going to let someone get away with threatening Tuck, let alone acting on the threat. "If you feel comfortable, Symeon, I think it's worth a shot." I looked over at Mart, and she was nodding.

"Me, too. But we have to be smart and careful." She looked up at him. "Nothing can happen to you."

We must have reached Jared's breaking point because he came back, slipped his arm through mine again, and said, "You are now a temporary deputy, sir. Meet me at my house in the morning to get fitted up for your surveillance job." He didn't look happy, but I knew he'd be even more unhappy if he knew something was going on, found out Symeon had been hurt, and realized he could have helped.

"And what about Tuck?" I asked.

"This is my investigation. Tuck has enough to handle with Catherine Birmingham's murder. We'll keep this between us." Jared's voice was firm, but the small frown lines by his mouth told me he didn't feel completely comfortable with the situation. But then, none of us did.

"Okay. Thanks, Jared," Symeon said. "I'll contact Dooley first thing tomorrow before my shift."

"And after you go by Jared's to get proper training," Mart added.

Symeon leaned over and kissed her quickly. "Of course."

THE NEXT MORNING, I was up early because Mart and I had decided we were going to Jared's to help Symeon, too. The guys had dropped us off last night and then headed home themselves, and while Mart and I were really tempted to indulge in some late-night TV, we both went to bed instead since we knew we needed to be rested for our stake out.

That's what we'd decided to call Symeon's undercover mission, even though it didn't involve sitting somewhere and watching anyone, much less running out for coffee at just the moment something goes down, like it always did in the TV shows. Plus, in my head I was calling it the "Steak Out" and wondering why no one had opened a restaurant with that name.

I got showered and dressed and then went into the kitchen to make buckwheat pancakes for Mart and me. It was a chilly morning, just above freezing, and I figured we'd need good, weighty food in our bellies for both the walk to Jared's and the need to brace ourselves for Symeon's first foray into the racist's den.

I took out the maple syrup from the fridge, poured a bit into a saucepan, and slowly warmed it over the stove. Then, I scooped a big chunk of butter out of the butter bell, mixed in a bit of cinnamon, and set it on the table. Finally, I washed some blueberries and slipped them into a bowl.

By the time Mart came out a few minutes later, breakfast was ready, the kitchen smelled heavenly, and the act of cooking had calmed my nerves a bit. "Oh, Harvey, thank you," she said as she sat down heavily at the table. "I'm so nervous."

I sighed. "I am, too." I knew a bit about what it was like for someone you loved to be in harm's way – it was one of the hardest things about Jared's job for me. "He's going to be okay. Jared will train him well."

Mart reached over and squeezed my hand as I sat down next to her. "Thanks. Now, tell me about breakfast."

I smiled and walked her through what I had made. "I only made a half batch of pancakes, though, because if we eat too much buckwheat, we'll have to let our overstuffed bellies lead us down the street."

"I'm not sure we need to worry about having any leftovers," Mart said as she looked under the table to see Taco and Mayhem waiting not so patiently for anything we might drop.

THE STROLL to Jared's house was invigorating both because of the crisp fall air and the enthusiastic chasing of squirrels that the dogs seemed intent on this morning. Mart and I each held one leash, and then we just let the dogs lead us to-and-fro as we walked the quiet streets – sometimes in the street itself instead of on the sidewalk. I was glad we had lived here for a while so that people knew it was only our love of dogs, not an affection for early morning cocktails, that gave us our weaving steps.

When we got to Jared's house, the men met us on the front porch with coffee and scones. I almost groaned audibly when I saw that they were my favorite – chocolate chip – but then I realized that even buckwheat pancakes – heavy as they are – metabolize quickly. I was indeed able to eat again, and I didn't hesitate.

The coffee was dark and rich, and the scone just sweet enough to be perfect, somewhere between biscuit and cookie. And the company was perfect. We were all a bit giddy given our upcoming subterfuge, and between our nervous jokes about Symeon as Billy Bob, the undercover Good Ole Boy and the copious amounts of caffeine we had all ingested, we were practically crying with laughter as Jared applied the wire he'd borrowed from work to Symeon's chest.

"Now, when you take it off," Jared said as he pressed the body glue into Symeon's chest hair, " try soap and water first. Don't just pull it off. If it hurts too much after you wash it, use some Vaseline and let it soak in."

"What? – A bald patch between my pecks isn't sexy?" Symeon said with a laugh.

"I'll be the judge of that," Mart quipped, "but let's not make me have to decide, okay?"

"Fair enough," Symeon said and kissed the top of her head.

Things got more serious when Jared started talking about code words and such. If Symeon needed Jared, he was to talk about wanting to get a dog, a French Bulldog specifically. Symeon loved dogs and did indeed want one, but he was more of a Bernese Mountain Dog kind of guy than a French Bulldog. But Jared wanted something just a little outside of natural for Symeon to say if he needed intervention.

The more Jared talked about how he would be right over if something went wrong, the more nervous I got. In my mind, I was just seeing a political office, like something off *Parks and Rec* maybe, and a bunch of people sitting around and making phone calls. I wasn't sure what exactly would require a code word for extrication. Finally, my nerves got the better of me, and I blurted, "Do we really need this? I mean they're a bunch of politicians."

Jared looked at me, and his gaze softened. "It's intense, I know, but we are in Octonia County, where most everyone and their cousin has a gun of some sort. And these are the people we suspect of threatening our sheriff's life if he doesn't pull out of the election."

This little speech wasn't helping to ease my nerves, but I knew Jared was reminding me of the truth. And with his reminder came a flash of understanding. "You think these guys might be part of a hate group, don't you?"

Jared's face clouded over as he nodded. "Identity Dixie has been active around here for some time, and we have some evidence that Dooley is involved, maybe very involved."

My heart was racing, and when I looked over at Mart, I saw all the color had drained from her face.

"Maybe this is a bad idea," she said.

Symeon had gotten very still, but he shook his head. "I need to do this more than ever then. They were down in Charlottesville for August twelfth, weren't they?"

Jared nodded, "And they have organized a few other rallies. They are white supremacist and misogynistic to the extreme. Scary folks."

I took Mart's hand and said, "I'm with Mart. Maybe we need to back off."

Symeon stood up and shook his head again. "Nope. I'm a red-headed, Irish-rooted man, and these men give me a bad name, and if they hate my friends and believe the woman I love needs me to tell her what to do," Mart sucked in a breath at that statement, "then I need to be a part of taking them down."

I squeezed Mart's fingers and then pushed her to stand up. "You love me?" she whispered.

"Of course, I do," he said as he kissed her. "I'll be safe, okay? French bulldogs are my favorite." He winked at her and then walked down the porch steps. "See you all soon."

For a split second, Mart just watched him walk away, but then, she sprinted off the porch, turned him around, whispered something in his ear, and then kissed him so hard I turned away to give them privacy.

As Symeon resumed his walk, I could see that the tips of his ears were red, and there was a good blush on Mart's face when she returned to the porch . . . but the color drained away quickly as she looked at Jared. "He will be safe, right?"

"I will keep him safe, but that means I need to focus." He leaned over and kissed my cheek. "See you tonight?"

"Absolutely, and you'll—"

"I'll let you know if I hear anything you need to hear," he said without letting me finish. Then he stood, put on his belt with gun and radio, and walked to his car with a small ear piece in his right ear. "I've got him," he said again before he climbed into the car.

I stepped over and put my arm around Mart. "You're coming to work with me today," I said. She had been planning to go to her office and catch up on paperwork, but if I was in her position, the last thing I'd want is to be alone, doing monotonous tasks while my boyfriend was potentially risking his life. "We'll go back your office and get what you need."

I knew she was worried because she didn't even put up her usual "I'm fine" front for me to break through. She just nodded and let me guide her back to our house and my car.

WE WERE out to the winery where Mart worked and back to my shop with a few minutes to spare before we opened. With Mart's help, I did the very few things needed to get the store open because, of course, Marcus had prepped everything the night before, and when I unlocked the door and turned on the sign, there was already a crowd of folks waiting.

I had really underestimated the traffic that those last-minute Harrow tickets were generating, but I made a note to try this tactic for any future events. If this many people would come into my store for a chance to win something that cost me nothing, I figured I could probably manage this strategy each time someone came to read.

Many of those who came to enter also scooped up copies of Harrow's books, sometimes all of the titles, and others headed to the café for their morning caffeination. Still others seemed

surprised to find a quaint, well-stocked bookstore when they
came in, or at least that's how I interpreted their smiles and
slower steps as they came in and looked around. More than one
new face spent some time browsing as I rang up books and
answered questions.

One woman who looked to be about sixty with rosy cheeks,
creamy skin and green spiked hair was looking for cozy
mysteries that featured women who were older than forty,
confident, and could "kick ass" in some way. I immediately
thought of all the heroines in Ellery Adams' books, but I
recommended *Murder In the Mystery Suite* specifically because I
thought she'd appreciate how Jane is both a hotel manager *and*
a guardian of a great secret. She picked up that title and the rest
of the series, too, paid for her books, and then headed to the
café to start reading.

When I saw her with a cinnamon roll, a latte, and twenty
pages of the first book behind her, I figured we had a new
customer for life. And when we had a lull in customers, I
followed suit behind her, bought Mart and me two cinnamon
rolls, and joined her at her small table.

She had stacks of paper spread around her, but as best I
could tell, she was simply staring out the window and chewing
on the end of her hair. It was a nervous habit she'd had, she
told me once, since she was in fifth grade and Davy Mackey and
called her a cry baby on the playground. She'd pulled her hair
into her mouth to hide the fact that she was indeed crying and
the habit had stuck. It was her way of managing nervous energy
and shielding herself from anyone who might notice her
nerves.

Her shield was working so well that day that when I sat
down across from her, she actually jumped in surprise, even
though she'd been facing me as I walked up. "Oh, Mart," I said
as I set the warm, home-baked roll in front of her. "How can I
help?"

She shook her head and sighed. "This helps," she said as she picked up her fork and proceeded to poke an elaborate pattern in the top of her roll without taking a bite.

"Remember that Jared said no news is good news," I said as I put my hand over hers. "I haven't heard from him, have you?"

She shook her head. "But what if no news means Jared thinks there's no news but really Symeon is tied to a chair and being beaten up to find out what he knows?"

I stared at her a minute and then shook my head. "Mart, why in the world would politicians do that? And besides, Symeon doesn't know anything. He can't even act shifty because he doesn't have anything to hide."

Mart pulled her hands down her face and looked up at me. "I'm being a little dramatic, aren't I?"

"I think what you're doing is letting your anxiety manifest as catastrophic thinking," I said.

Mart cracked a smile. "You've been reading self-help books again."

I shrugged. "It's a side effect of the job. I realize something about myself, and then I have an infinite number of resources to learn more."

"So what has your reading about anxiety told you?" She said as she leaned back and crossed her arms.

I took a big bite of my cinnamon roll and then after I chewed, I said. "You know it's totally reasonable to be worried, right?"

Mart let her head fall back over the top of her chair. "I do. But I hate feeling this way. It's so powerless."

I understood exactly what she meant. Some of the reason I'd been reading about anxiety is that I noticed I started getting very edgy and nervous when I didn't hear from Jared for some period of time that I thought, for whatever reason, was too long. I quickly imagined the worst – from him being shot in the line of duty to him deciding he had made a mistake and didn't really care about me.

"Yep, I get it. We are powerless right now, but Jared's not. And Symeon's not either. And we trust them, right?" I leaned forward and grabbed her hand.

She lifted her head and looked at me. "We do," she said quietly and then repeated. "We do. They're smart, capable men."

At that exact moment, my phone pinged. I looked down to see Jared's name on the display. "It's Jared," I said as I scooped up the phone and opened his message.

Mart craned forward to read my screen. "What does it say?"

"Symeon's on his way over. He's fine," I said as I looked up at her and saw the tears well in her eyes. "He's fine."

She nodded and then picked up her fork. "Now, I can finally eat this thing."

As Mart ate and moaned, a little excessively, over her cinnamon roll, I read the rest of Jared's message that said we needed to meet Symeon at the back door of the shop since he was going to slip through Max's restaurant first just to keep things looking as normal as possible and try to avoid connecting himself with me if he could.

A few minutes later, we stood at the back of the shop pacing until we heard a light rap on the door. Mart opened the door, scooted Symeon into the back room, and then hugged him so tight I'm pretty sure I heard his spine crack. While they "connected," I cleared off the staff lunch table, made sure we had four chairs, and then sat down to peruse our inventory on my phone while we waited for Jared.

Fortunately, he arrived quickly because I was seeing, much to my disappointment, that our inventory of Harrow's books was already markedly low, and I was going to need to place a last minute order to be shipped overnight. I'd have to get that order in right away to be sure they arrived in time, but right now, I needed to focus on what Symeon had to say.

"I don't have anything yet," he began, "but I think they trust me. They asked if I wanted to do a bit of campaigning this afternoon, and I said yes, once I checked in with my boss."

Jared asked, "You've let Max know what you're doing?"

I studied Jared's face because I wasn't sure what he wanted Symeon's answer to be.

"I have," Symeon said, "or kind of. I told him I was helping you with something to do with the murder."

"That's good. We don't want him worrying or asking questions, but also, it's best if no one else know exactly what is going on."

"Does Tuck know?" Mart asked.

Jared shrugged. "Sort of. I told him I had a CI in Dooley's office, but he doesn't know it's you."

I frowned. "I know you want to protect him and let him focus on solving Catherine's murder, but he is the sheriff. Doesn't he need to know?"

"Maybe. In time. But right now, we don't know anything new to tell him." He looked over at Symeon. "Right?"

"Right," Symeon said. "I do know the men – and they were all men – who were there today don't have any love lost for Tuck." He grimaced. "And the way they talked about their wives? It was disgusting."

I shivered. Ever since I realized there were men who didn't share lascivious quips about women, I'd made sure I only spent time with men who respected us. It had taken me far too long to realize there were those men, though.

"Alright, so keep the wire on. I'll patrol this afternoon so that I'm able to respond if you need me. But you will have to keep me posted about where you are, okay? I can't follow in my cruiser without getting spotted." Jared held Symeon's gaze until the chef nodded.

"Sounds good. Now, I really do have to go to work. Lunch services starts," he looked at his watch, "in fifteen." He stood up, gave Mart another quick hug, and then headed out, through the back door again.

Jared, Mart, and I wandered to the front of the store, and I thought about asking Jared, again, if we were doing the right thing. But I knew that question would only make all of us more antsy, and it might also make Jared think I didn't trust him.

So instead, I said, "I have to order more books. Want to help?" I looked at the two of them, and they both nodded. "Follow me."

The truth was that I didn't have much of a way for them to help me since I simply had to go into my distributor's page, punch in the quantity of each title I wanted, and pay for them. But from the way Mart and Jared were both lingering near me, I thought they probably needed a little distraction. I sent them to count the numbers of each title of Harrow's that we still had. Technically, I could see these numbers in my inventory system, but given that someone might have stolen a couple, I thought I could explain myself if anyone thought to ask about why we were doing a manual count.

As they began to count and write down numbers, Marcus came in to begin his shift. He gave Jared and Mart a quick glance, looked at me, and then said, "We're in the thick of it again, aren't we?"

I sighed. Marcus was one of the most perceptive people I knew. "Yeah, Symeon is undercover with Dooley's campaign. "They're both worried, so I'm trying to keep them busy."

"Got it. Think Mart wants to help me redo the front window?" he asked as he slipped his backpack under the register. "I have an idea."

"I'm sure she would, and maybe I can order in some subs

for all of us." I took out my phone and pulled up the food delivery app to take Marcus's order then headed around to gather Rocky's, Mart's, and Jared's. The sub shop was just up the road, so our food would be here in 15 minutes. Just enough time for Jared and Mart to finish counting titles.

Meanwhile, I prepped the order I thought I needed so I could confirm it against their count, and when they were done, I put in my order with assurances, by phone from the distributor, that everything would be definitely be here tomorrow.

When the subs arrived, Mart, Jared, and I headed out first to eat ours on the bench in front of the store. My first instinct was to avoid that place given that two days before someone had been killed while I sat there, but I knew that the only way I'd have new associations with that seat was to sit there and build new ones.

As we ate, Jared asked Mart about our trip to meet The Rock the next week. He asked her all kinds of things she couldn't possibly know – how many horses did he have? How many acres? Did he have a staff? – and I knew, as I expect Mart did, that he was just trying to keep her thoughts on something other than the fact that her boyfriend was about to get into a vehicle with men who had, almost certainly, threatened our friend's life.

The distraction could only last so long, though, because about one o'clock, we saw Symeon head down the street and climb into the cab of a huge black pickup. He was on his way, and that meant Jared needed to head out, too. He gave me a quick kiss, gathered up all our trash for the trashcan, and then jogged up the street to where his cruiser was parked.

I hoped no one was watching him or if they were, they thought maybe he was just running late for his shift. It wasn't exactly normal Main Street with a police officer running up the sidewalk.

With lunch done and the intensity of the day only ramping

up, I figured both Mart and I could use the distraction of a
window display. So while Marcus finished up his lunch, we
gathered titles for his new "Witches and Warlocks" window. It
was a perfect idea to feature during Harrow's reading, given her
book *Once and Future Witches*, and it also blended with
Halloween and the "Haunted Bookstore" event we had planned
for kids at the end of the month.

Marcus had made a list of titles he wanted to include, and
so we gathered those first. *Practical Magic* by Alice Hoffman
headed his list, so we gathered it and the other titles in that
series. Then we grabbed *The Hazel Wood* by Melissa Albert, *The
Black Prism* by Brent Weeks, and *The Last Wish*, the first book in
the popular Witcher series. I threw in one of my favorites,
Garden Spells by Sarah Addison Allen, and Mart selected the
classic play, *The Crucible*.

By the time Marcus was ready to hang the giant witch's hat
Rocky had cut out of poster board, we had all the books as well
as some tree branches that had dropped behind the store to
add to his display. Soon, the front windows were full of magic –
both literary and visual – as Marcus did his thing to tie the
giant display of Harrow's book, which was beginning to grow a
bit meager as we stole from it to stock the floor, with his new
witch arrangement.

Mart found some old yarn in the back room and wove an
elaborate spiderweb in one corner, and Rocky recruited a
couple of teenagers who dropped by after school to carve some
witchy jack-o-lanterns. Add to that the fog machine that
Marcus had rented for the weekend, and the entire front of the
store looked downright creepy and mystical.

Fortunately, the work had been pretty engrossing for all of
us, and between that and handling customer needs, we
managed to pass most of the afternoon without too much angst
on Mart's part. Jared updated me every half-hour or so to say
there was nothing to worry about and that he was staying close

but not too close to where Symeon was since Symeon was doing a stellar job of communicating where the truck was.

But I didn't tell Mart anything, preferring to let her focus and be distracted rather than pushing her mind to her worries again and again. I would definitely have told her if something was wrong, but since nothing was, I just let the time pass.

5

Finally, as dusk began to settle and my shift at the store came to an end, Jared said Symeon was headed back to work and suggested we all meet there. As soon as I told Mart the plan, she bolted out the back door. I ran close behind and took a minute to explain the situation to a surprised Max when she breezed past him to reach Symeon as he came into the kitchen.

Max was gracious and allowed us to use the chef's table in the kitchen to debrief on Symeon's afternoon even as Symeon began prepping the dinner service. His sous-chef wouldn't be in for a half-hour, he said, so he had a little time to fill us in.

"So basically, we drove around, talked to people about Dooley, and put out some signs," Symeon said to begin. "We were campaigning, like they said."

Jared sighed. "So nothing to report again?"

"I didn't say that," Symeon said with a sly grin as he managed to chop a dozen onions without shedding a single tear. "We did make one interesting stop. You know that old lodge off Brandt Road, the one made of cinder blocks?"

I shook my head, but Mart and Jared nodded. "Basketball

hoop outside? Playground out back? I always thought that was a church," Jared said.

"Me, too," Symeon replied as he tossed the onions and some minced garlic into a huge sauce pan filled with olive oil. "But it's actually the local Identity Dixie headquarters."

"What?!" Jared said. "How do you know? Did you go inside?"

Symeon shook his head. "No, they told me to wait in the car, but I made like I had to pee and walked around the outside of the building so I could peek in the windows. Nazi flags, Confederate Flags everywhere."

I shuddered. "Creepy."

"Very," Symeon said. "I tried to ask, casually, when we were back in the truck, about what that place was, but the guy driving, Ricky, would only say that I might get an invite at some point if I kept up the good work."

Jared sighed. "Well, that's good to know. We can keep an eye on the place. Nice work, Symeon." He put out his hand. "Now, I should get that wire back to the station."

Symeon stopped stirring the onions and looked at Jared. "What do you mean? I haven't learned anything yet. I'm not done."

I flashed a worried look at Jared and then at Mart, thinking she'd be frowning because of what Symeon said. Instead, she was smiling.

"That's my man," she whispered just loudly enough for me to hear. "You're so brave," she said to him.

"Symeon, I don't think this is a good idea," Jared said. "The more times you go in, the more risk there is for you."

"I know that," Symeon said as he turned to the opposite counter and began slicing carrots into the thinnest pieces I'd ever seen. "But the more I go in, the more they can also come to trust me. Maybe I can find out who is threatening Tuck."

Mart said, "I'm not thrilled about the risk either, but we need to make some headway."

Just then, Max came through the swinging door from the dining room. "Symeon, a table of six has just come in. They said they are friends of yours." Something about the look of skepticism on Max's face made me curious.

Symeon stepped to the window in the door and peered out. "It's the guys from today, or at least five of them are. The sixth guy I don't know." He took off his apron. "Guess I better go say hi."

My stomach tightened. They had come here to see Symeon, probably to check out his story, and if we had slipped and gone out through the front . . . I couldn't even think about it.

Max looked from me to Jared and then to Mart. "It's probably a good idea for someone to tell me more about what's going on here," he said.

Jared sighed. "Yeah, okay." He filled Max in on the threat to Tuck's life, Catherine's murder, and Symeon's undercover operation. "The guys who came in are Dooley's men."

"And Dooley," Max added. "I recognize him from the ads I keep getting in my mailbox." He shook his head. "Not sure how I got on *that* list."

I chuckled. Max and I had a good if very casual friendship now after a rocky start to our relationship, then a brief romance, and now a passing friendship based on those hard things. I turned to Jared. "So what do we do?"

"Well, Max, how do you feel about eavesdropping on your customers?" Jared asked.

A glint came into Max's eye. "Normally, I try to be the pinnacle of discretion, but when white supremacist hate groups are concerned, I figure they've foregone their right to even the semblance of privacy." He grinned. "I'll keep an ear open and stay as close as I can. It'll be a bonus if I can be so over-attentive that they never come back."

I laughed. "I like this plan."

"Me, too," Jared said. "Symeon will be able to tell us who the men are, well, most of them. You recognize anyone else?" he asked Max.

"Nope, just Dooley."

I slipped over to the window and peered through. I couldn't see the men very well since they were across the room and the lighting was dim for the evening service, but I didn't think I recognized anyone. Then, I gasped. One of the men had stood and was walking toward the back of the restaurant. "Roger Birmingham," I whispered.

"Who's Roger Birmingham?" Max sad quietly from just over my shoulder.

"The victim's father," Jared said near my other ear.

The three of us tried to peer out the tiny porthole-sized window in the door, but there wasn't much else to see. When Symeon started back this way, we darted back, and I grabbed Mart's hand. She was staring at the door, lost in thought.

Symeon swung the door open carefully and slipped in, being sure that we couldn't be seen from the dining room. "So the one I didn't know was Bryan Dooley. I didn't meet him today. The other guys are all the ones who campaigned with us this afternoon."

"What?! Roger Birmingham is part of Identity Dixie," I said.

"Yeah, sure," Symeon said. "He's the guy I rode with today, seemed like me might be a leader of some sort." He was back to the range and pouring wine over risotto before he sliced mushrooms and added them to my favorite dish on Max's menu.

He said this so casually that I wasn't sure what to make of my own reaction. My heart was pounding, and my palms were sweaty. Instinctively, I went to stand beside Jared and let him comfort me. "That's Catherine's father," I told Symeon.

The chef stopped stirring and turned to me. "Are you serious?"

"Dead serious," I said. "Pun intended."

"Did he say anything about his daughter?" Jared asked.

Symeon turned back to the saucepan and resumed stirring. "Yeah, tons. He talked about her all afternoon, about what a good girl she was, about how she'd had her struggles but had been wonderful even then. He said she had died recently."

"Not that she was murdered," Mart asked.

"Not a word about that," Symeon said. "I just thought he was a guy who had lost his kid. He seemed pretty torn up about it all. Of course."

"Curiouser and curiouser," Jared said with a wink at me. He knew I took a thrill from any literary reference, especially one to *Alice In Wonderland*. "Did he say anything about what he thought had happened to her?"

Symeon shook his head. "So I really have to keep going," Symeon said as he put a lid over the risotto and mixed up a huge batch of ground beef with rosemary and blue cheese before sliding two burgers onto the grill. "Maybe we can find out something about Catherine's death while I'm there."

Jared let out an audible sigh. "Fine, but I'm going in, too."

I felt my heart slam against my tonsils. "What are you talking about? They'll know you are a cop."

"They will, but sadly, not all cops are above the law or really take serious their call to serve and protect. I've known enough of those folks to play the part." He turned to Symeon. "When do you meet with them again?"

"Tomorrow morning, early," Symeon said as he laid brioche buns on the grill that he'd just coated in butter. If I wasn't so worried, I would have been very hungry by this point.

"Tell them tonight that you're bringing me along. Sell me as best you can without looking like it." He looked at Symeon. "Be sure to tell them I'm a cop. Best to have that out in the open."

Symeon nodded, and I saw a look pass from him to Jared. They were enjoying the intrigue of this, and I got the sense that this was going to be one of those experiences that cemented their friendship. That is, if it didn't kill them.

I looked over at Mart, and her face was ashen. I wasn't exactly sure what she was thinking, but I wondered if she was regretting her support of Symeon's desire to stay undercover.

The orders started coming in from the front of house, so Symeon had to focus, so the three of us headed out. I felt a little conflicted at that moment because it was the night Jared and I usually had a date, but I also didn't want to leave Mart alone.

Jared must have had the same thought because he said, "Pizza and a movie, ladies," as he put out both his arms to us.

Mart took his right arm as I wrapped my hand around his left as we walked the few steps back to my store. "Thanks for the invite, Jared, but I have other plans," Mart said as she walked to the front of the store.

I followed her with the hopes of reassuring her that it was totally fine for us all to hang out, but I stopped short when my mom came through the door and gave Mart a hug. "You ready?" Mom said.

"Yep. I'm hoping you're going to go for passion fruit," Mart said with a smile.

"You never know. I'm feeling a little bit wild," Mom said as she turned to me. "Have a great date, Harvey. I'll get the scoop from Mart."

I looked from my mom to my best friend. "You two are going out?"

"I asked your mom to come with me to mani-pedi and dinner tonight. I didn't want to intrude on your date and didn't think it was smart for me to be alone." She wrapped her arm around Mom's shoulder. "Plus, I could use a little Mama time."

I grinned. Mart had lost her mom a few years earlier, and ever since we'd been friends, I'd told her that my mom thought of her as a daughter. It was good to see Mart taking that to heart and taking care of herself, too. "Have a blast, but I want photos."

"You got it," Mom said. "I've got a surprise for dinner, and it will warrant photos."

"Ooh," Mart said and then leaned over to hug me. "Thanks for loaning me your mom."

I hugged her tight. "Any time," I whispered and then watched them go.

Jared slipped up behind me and slipped his arms around my waist. "So what will it be tonight? Out or in?"

I leaned my head back against his chest. "Out. Someplace with great food, good beer, and dancing."

Jared spun me around. "Are you serious? *You* want to go dancing."

"Well," I said looking up at him through my eyelashes, "I want to go anywhere with you, but yeah, tonight, a couple of beers, some fried food, and some boot scootin' sound great."

With a sweep of his arms, Jared had me moving toward the door with the dogs in tow. "I know just the place."

We dropped Mayhem and Taco at home and left the back-door cracked so they could go in and out at will, just in case we were later than we planned. Then, we swung by Jared's house so he could change out of his uniform. When he came down the stairs in jeans, a flannel shirt, and boots, I whistled. He looked good – just the right blend of country boy and edgy. I could see the thin line of one of his tattoos peeking out of his sleeve. He was hot, and now my plan for the evening sounded even better.

I climbed into the cab of Jared's truck, and slid over to sit next to him. I hadn't done that since high school, but since there was a seatbelt in the middle of the bench seat and I was really looking forward to flirting with my boyfriend all night, I let myself regress just a bit. Jared grinned, put his hand on my knee, and squeezed.

. . .

THE NIGHT WAS SO fun and just what both of us needed. We ate potato skins and drank moderately good beer, and we danced. Line danced. I had taken a line dancing course for my PE credit back in college, and I was surprised at how much I remember. But it was Jared who was the real star. Those boots had obviously seen the dance floor before.

When Jared took me home that night, I felt more at ease than I had in days, and I could see that a lot of the tension had slid off his shoulders, too. The long kiss he gave me at the door had my toes curling, and when I went inside to find Mart sound asleep on the couch with *Vampire Diaries* on the TV and a half-empty glass of wine on the coffee table, I decided tonight had been good for all of us.

I helped Mart to bed, made sure the dogs had water, and climbed into my covers with a smile.

Sleep came hard and fast, but when I heard Taco jump down from where he had, somehow, joined me, I woke up. *Maybe he just wanted to go back to the living room*, I thought.

But a moment later, both he and Mayhem lit up the house with their barks, and next to my head, Aslan went all angry cat with her back arched and her hiss on full force. Something had set them off.

Mart and I met in the hallway and exchanged a glance. She had grabbed the baseball bat that she keeps beside her door, and I was wielding a giant, heavy flashlight. Sadly, we had learned to be prepared for intruders.

The dogs were still barking with full gusto, so we followed the sound of them through the dark house until we saw them at the back door, hackles raised. No one in the neighborhood was sleeping well by this point, I was sure, so any element of surprise we'd had was gone. I flipped on the flood lights into the backyard as Mart raised her bat.

There, staring right at us through a black mask, was the largest raccoon I'd ever seen. He was sitting by our patio table with an apple from our compost bin in his mouth, and I swear it looked like he was smiling at the dogs.

I let out a rough exhale and felt Mart lower the bat. Then, we both looked at each other and started to laugh. Clearly, all of this had us on edge.

Our nearly hysterical laughter puzzled the pups as they looked from us to the racoon and back again. They had calmed a bit, but Mayhem was still letting her alert bark fly every few seconds. Taco, however, could smell the apple and had his tail going. He was ready to make friends if it meant he got a snack, I guess.

"I don't think we should let them out, do you?" I asked Mart.

She shook her head. "Nah, Rac-Rac is not doing any harm, and he may actually be sick. Better to keep them in."

"Rac-Rac?" I asked with a smile.

"It's what my stuffed racoon was named as a kid." She rolled her eyes. "No one said I was a creative preschooler."

I smiled and put my arm around her as I glanced over at the clock on the stove. Three-thirty a.m. "I'm going back to bed."

"Why bother if that one keeps going off like a fire alarm?" She pointed at Mayhem.

"Oh, I can fix that," I said and turned to the dogs. "Who wants to sleep in my bed?"

Both sets of ears swiveled and then they jogged off toward my room with nary a backward glance toward the animal outside.

"I'll have to remember that," Mart said. "But now, where are you going to sleep?"

"Wait for it," I said, and a second later, two hounds came charging back up the hall. "Aslan doesn't share well." I laughed as I walked over and grabbed the two dog beds from the fireplace.

"You're always one step ahead, Harvey Beckett. Always one step ahead." Mart slung her bat over her shoulder and made her way back to her room while I dragged the dog beds behind her.

Within seconds, both dogs and the cat were sound asleep and snoring. It sounded like a kazoo festival meets a freight train in my room, but, for better or worse, I found I wasn't sleepy anyway. I kept thinking about Roger Birmingham, about how much sympathy I had for him, about how I knew his grief was sincere when we talked. But I couldn't reconcile that tenderness with the fact that about how his grief had seemed so sincere but then how he was not only spending time with, but organizing, a group of verified white supremacists. I just couldn't reconcile those two ideas in my head, and my brain was spinning with the effort. I realized people were complex, and I knew everyone loved their children . . . but for me to figure out how to think about him, that's where I was struggling.

Finally, I paid attention to my body, realized I was getting more and more anxious, and forced myself to think about lovely things while I took long, deep breaths. I thought about dancing with Jared, about how nice it felt to have his hands on my hips, about watching him laugh across the booth from me earlier in the evening. And eventually, I drifted off to the symphony of pet breathing in my room.

6

The next morning, Mart and I were both silent at the peninsula in the kitchen as we ate cold cereal and tried not to think or talk about the fact that both of the men we loved were, as we shoveled in Count Chocula cereal, about to go into a situation that was potentially mortally dangerous.

Jared had texted at six a.m. to say they were on their way, and while I was awake and had been for quite a while, I let my phone sit until seven so that he didn't have to know how anxious I was.

But both Mart and I had been up for hours, and while we'd tried to keep busy for a while by tidying the house and even going so far as to vacuum and clean the bathrooms, we were now out of busy work. "I guess we just need to feel what we feel, huh?" I said between mouthfuls of sugar.

"I don't love feeling what I'm feeling just now," she said.

"Same. Same," I added. "So let's feel what we feel but not dwell on it, okay?"

Mart nodded. "Okay. So what are you doing today?"

I smiled. "I have to get the last of the details ready for Alix

Harrow." I had never been more excited to have an author in my store, and I really wanted everything to be perfect. "What about you?"

"Fortunately, my bosses are hosting a major event this afternoon, so I'll be busy setting up and prepping the staff," she said with a glance at her phone on the counter.

'But you won't be too busy to step out if need be." I had been thinking much the same thing since Marcus had planned to come in today. I really wanted to be at work and get things done, but if Jared needed me, I could leave at a moment's notice.

"Exactly," Mart said. "So what do you say we do a little drive by that lodge place before I drop you off?"

I stood up, put on my scarf, and slipped my arm around her shoulder. "This is one of the many reasons I love you. You read my mind."

The dogs were, as always, ready to go, and while Aslan would have preferred I stay around to be her day-long cushion between feedings of tuna, she did give me a little leg rub before going nose first into the fresh food I put out for her. "You keep the house safe, girl," I said as I rubbed her chin and got an intense side eye for my effort.

With Mayhem and Taco in the back of Mart's car, we headed out of town and down the peninsula to the sideroad where Symeon had said the lodge was. Fortunately for us, the street was a main cut-through between the major north-south corridors, so traffic was pretty consistent. Around here, everyone knew everyone and what everyone drove, so we needed the cover of traffic to blend in.

As we approached the building, Mart slowed just slightly, and we turned to study the nondescript block of concrete as we drove past. The gravel parking lot was full of vehicles, and I picked out Symeon's sedan near the front. Jared had ridden with him to give them a chance to talk over their plans. They knew it was a risk since if they wouldn't let Jared in they would probably refuse Symeon again, despite his invitation. But we had insisted they go together. At least they'd have each other then.

I'd known it was going to be pretty fruitless to scope out the place, but sometimes, it just helps to see something. In this case, however, it didn't help because we didn't see anything we hadn't already seen dozens of times as we traveled around.

Plus, the lot was full, and my fantasies of it being a couple of sick, elderly men with our two, fit middle-aged guys were exploded. Now, I was more nervous than ever.

Mart drove on past the building and took the wide loop up north and then back west on another road before parking in front of my shop. "Well, that was disappointing."

I nodded. "But if all else fails, we can tell Tuck," I said even as I hoped that we had a lot of option before all else failed.

"True," Mart said, "and your mom is pretty fierce in a fight, I hear."

I jerked my head to stare at my friend. "What in the world are you talking about?"

Mart grinned. "She got a little tipsy last night and told me about a time she pinned a boy to his locker for touching her friend Mary without her permission. Apparently, he was totally surprised since your mom is so tiny."

I stared out the windshield for a minute and tried to picture my mom as a sixteen-year-old taking down a teenage boy. It wasn't actually that hard to picture. She had once carried me out of a Roses by one arm when I threw a fit about them not having my favorite kind of pencils. I was twelve.

"Good point. I'll loop her in," I said as I opened the door. "You hear anything . . ."

"I'll call right away – and back at you."

"Of course." I watched her drive away just to be sure she was really okay, but when she didn't hit a parked car or bounce over a curb, I figured she was alright and headed to the shop. It was no surprise that both Rocky and Marcus were already there, but I was a little puzzled to find Stephen and Walter setting up a small table with a luxurious rust-colored table cloth at the edge of the café.

"What's this?" I asked as I unleashed the dogs and then hugged my two friends.

"Well, we had an idea that we thought you'd like, and Marcus gave us permission to try it out." Stephen looked a little wary as he watched my face.

"Okay, so what's the idea?"

"We're collecting donations for an organization called Coming to the Table." Walter said. "Heard of them?"

I shook my head. "What do they do?"

"They're an anti-racist organization that helps connect the descendants of people who were enslaved with the descendants of the people who enslaved them," Stephen said.

"Whoa," I whispered. "That sounds intense."

"It is," Walter added, "but they do good work, and they're small, mostly volunteers. We're thinking of starting a local group, so if we raise enough money today, we'll split what we make with the national organization and start a new nonprofit for the rest here."

"Sign me up," I said, "for both a donation and the local group." I looked around at the store, which was immaculate. "Give me a quick run-down, and I'll steer people your way."

The guys filled me in on the organization's mission and gave me a few brochures to hand out, and then I went back to my opening chores, grateful for the small crowd that was waiting outside. It looked like it was going to be a busy day, and I needed all the distraction I could get.

I had already looked at my phone about eighty-seven times, but of course there was no word. I realized this was a good thing – no word meant nothing had gone wrong and the guys were still "in," but still my heartrate was rising and my chest tightening.

With five minutes before opening, I stepped into the back room, sat down at the staff table, and focused on my breath. Steady inhales and longer exhales. I counted as I breathed, and I tried to just focus on the way the table felt cool under my hands and the chair hard under my tush.

Meditation was not something I took to naturally. Even when I wasn't anxious, my brain spun about a mile a minute, but when that tightness reached my chest, my thoughts turned to spirals about what I didn't know but only imagined. Today was a bad day for that to happen, so I forced myself to let those thoughts go by and stayed with my breath.

It took a minute or two, but eventually, I felt the vise in my chest release a little, and my heart started to slow down. I took one more deep breath and then reminded myself that "thoughts are not things," the little mantra I'd given myself when I started to imagine that what I thought was truth.

Then, I went back on the floor, gave Marcus the nod, and began to greet the customers as they came in.

It was a blessedly busy morning. Between helping customers, talking with Harrow's publicist about details for tomorrow, sitting with Galen for a short BookTok interview about why I loved Harrow's books so much, and keeping the store as tidy as possible, I barely had time to think, much less worry.

I spent some time with a young mother whose toddler was enjoying a copy of *Where The Wild Things Are* and laughing at all the monsters. She wanted to get him some books that helped him "meet" people of other cultures and life experiences but that weren't about that expressly. "In my life, I've learned to understand the way people life by being friends with them rather than studying them. I'd like Ethan to have that chance, too."

I smiled. "Oh, then I have books for you." I headed to the picture book shelves as Ethan giggled again at the wild rumpus and began selecting titles. I handed her a dozen books, all my favorites and all about people who some considered different including *The Most Beautiful Thing* by Kao Kalia Young, *Sulwe* by Lupita Nyong'o, and *The Boy With Big Feelings* by Britney Winn Lee.

As Ethan continued to "read," she sat down at our amphitheater and followed suit. Soon, she was smiling and turning pages as she ran her fingers over some of the most gorgeous illustrations I knew. I watched her a moment and then headed back onto the main floor, confident she'd find just what she and Ethan needed.

Galen was still browsing the mystery shelves after our interview, so I took a second to swing by and give his Bulldog Mac a snuggle. Mac had been present for our interview, of course, but I hadn't been able to get my face into those ruffles around his neck like I wanted. Now, I sat down, snuffled up against him, and felt him collapse into my lap. Mac was probably the best canine snuggler I knew, but don't tell Mayhem or Taco. They'd be jealous.

As I petted Mac's loose skin and listened to him moan in delight, Galen smiled down above his armful of new titles. "You read this one?" he said and held up *Body in the Attic*.

I shook my head. "You?"

He smiled. Not yet, but I'll let you know." He shifted his stack and said, "I hate to bother you two, but do you mind ringing me up?"

I looked down at Mac. "I don't know, Mac. Do you think we can help your boss here?"

Mac stood and shook thoroughly.

"I'll take that as a yes," as I pulled myself to my feet and led the way to the register, where Marcus was handling the line of customers. I patted Galen on the shoulder and then spoke to everyone in line, trying to help ease the discomfort of the wait.

I'd been thinking about getting a second register for busy days and, today, it was clear I needed to do just that. I didn't want people to have to wait to get to their reading, and while Rocky could ring up sales now that we'd loaded my software to her register in the café, she was often busy enough to not make that any faster.

I glanced over at her, and sure enough, she had a line three people deep. It was clearly time to get a new machine. I stepped away from the line to make myself a voice note to see if I could get something delivered overnight so that we had two registers for Harrow's event, in case people wanted to buy.

Stephen and Walter had a steady stream of folks stopping by their table, which was no surprise given how charismatic my friends were and how deeply committed to justice many of the residents and guests in St. Marin's were. Every time we'd done a fundraiser for an organization that we believed in or that had helped someone we loved, the community had stepped up and helped us surpass our goal. I didn't know what kind of funds Stephen and Walter wanted to raise today, but I had no doubt they'd hit the goal and then some.

I was just about to step into the witchy front window and see what needed to be filled back in or moved to the floor for sale when the door to the shop swung open hard and a group of white men poured in. Most of them were in casual clothes, jeans, some camo pants, but a couple had on suits or more business-like attire. It wasn't often that we had groups of middle-aged guys coming into the store – bookstores weren't usually their scene – so I was puzzled enough by their arrival that it took me a minute to realize that Jared and Symeon were among them.

Jared caught my eye for the shortest second, gave his head a quick jerk to signal "No," and then moved right past me. Behind him a short, thin man in a gorgeous, tailored blue suit approached me as he slid the single lock of blonde hair that had fallen onto his forehead back into place. "I'm Bryan Dooley," he said. "Thanks for letting us take a break from campaigning to enjoy your store."

I stared at his extended hand for just a minute, but then I pulled myself together and shook his fingers. His grip was firm, but his hands were soft in a way that told me he didn't do a lot of physical labor. I didn't love that since even I, with my bookish self, had callouses on my palms from carrying boxes of books.

"Nice to meet you, Mr. Dooley. You're running for sheriff?" I asked, trying to play the part of informed but not overly informed citizen.

"That's right. I hope I can count on your vote," he said with a grin that would light up a stage or burn paint off a wall.

Fortunately before I had to figure out an answer, Marcus approached from behind and put his hand on my shoulder. "Harvey, Harrow's publicist is on the line again. I think you'll want to take this, maybe in the back room so you can focus." He held my gaze an extra second to be sure I understood.

I glanced back at Marcus, who had a placid expression on his face, but I could see the tightness in his jaw as he turned to greet Dooley. "I'm sorry to interrupt, but maybe I can help you."

Dooley's smile only faltered for a split second as he looked at my African American assistant manager, but I knew that even that tiny slip wouldn't get past Marcus. I also knew that Marcus was, unfortunately, used to people who thought him lesser because of the color of his skin, so I walked toward the back room glad to see that Galen was still shopping and Rocky had an eye on her boyfriend.

As I passed the history section, I saw Symeon and Roger Birmingham, who had slipped past my notice earlier apparently, standing with their eyes bent over a book. I couldn't see what title it was, but from the scowl of derision on Birmingham's face, I figured he wasn't pleased with the book's message.

I stepped into the back room quickly and closed the door. There, tucked into the corner behind the door was Jared, and he was smiling. He gestured me over and pulled me into a big hug. "Sorry I couldn't give you a heads up. Dooley decided to stop on a whim, said he'd heard about you and your store and wanted to pay a visit to 'drum up some support.'"

I rolled my eyes. "Does he think a little glad-handing will make me take Tuck's sign out of the window?"

Jared sighed. "Oh, I doubt that. From what I've seen today, this is more about intimidation than about actual campaigning. We've spent the morning going door to door at all the houses with Tuck's signs in the yard. As you can imagine, it's no casual thing for fifteen white guys to approach your house."

I shivered. "Just the thought makes me antsy. I can't imagine if I was home alone with kids or a person of color." I let that idea flit through my mind for a moment as I imagined the men marching toward someone's front door, but then a terrible thought occurred to me. "Wait, all those people saw you with Dooley."

He nodded. "It's going to take some major explaining to clarify the situation to folks, but I did decide to clue Tuck in this morning before we went into the lodge. So I expect he's already doing damage control."

A little more ease slipped into my chest at the news that the sheriff knew where Jared and Symeon were today. "What made you decide that?"

Jared tugged me close again. "You. I didn't want you worrying all day without word. Tuck was going to come by at lunch and let you know he was on top of the situation."

I slid my face into his neck and kissed it. "Thank you. I've been trying to keep my mind off things, but it wasn't always working."

He rubbed small circles on my back. "I have to get back out there. But I don't think you have any reason to worry. It doesn't seem like Dooley has any idea that Symeon and I aren't really there to support him."

"Okay, good. Keep it that way, alright?" I pulled back and looked up at him. "Any leads on who threatened Tuck?"

Jared shook his head. "Not yet, but Birmingham and Symeon have gotten pretty tight. I'm hoping Sy might know more. Maybe he learned something about Catherine that will be helpful, too."

I grinned. "Sy, huh?"

"You go undercover with a man, you get close quick," he said before he bent to give me a gentle kiss and then signaled for me to go ahead of him.

I stepped out of the back room a few moments later and headed toward the restroom to check supplies and use the facilities. As I turned the corner out of the back hallway, I almost walked into Roger Birmingham, who was staring back down the hall from which I'd just come. "Oh, hi Mr. Birmingham. Good to see you again."

His eyes shifted to my face, and his gaze softened. "Oh, hi. Good to see you." He slipped his eyes back to the hall. "What's back there?"

Alarm bells went off in my head. "Back door," I said quickly, hoping that at least that might give Jared a plausible reason to have been back that way.

Birmingham glanced at me and then smiled again. "Ah, right. Makes sense." He patted my arm and then turned back toward the front of the store, where I could see Dooley's men beginning to gather again.

I continued to the bathroom, slipped into a stall, and texted Jared about Birmingham watching the back hall. I took a few minutes to tidy up and replace toilet paper and paper towels, hoping Jared might text back, but when my phone stayed quiet, I stepped back onto the floor and went in search of Marcus.

He was at the register, ringing up a copy of *Mein Kämpf* for one of Dooley's men. I sold the book because it told an important piece of history, one that it behooved us to heed. But in this guy's hands, I didn't think the book would be read as a cautionary tale, and the thought made my stomach turn, especially as I saw Marcus's brown hand slip it into a bag.

Once the man caught up to his group, which was now milling about outside, I turned to Marcus. "Are you okay?"

He shrugged. "No, but I'm not any more un-okay than I am sometimes. None of those guys were outright ugly, but it's the subtle things – the looks, the extra steps to avoid my path, the time to double-check that I gave back the right change – those things add up. " He sighed. "I'm going to go take a break in the café if you're alright here."

"Of course. I'll call for you if I need you." I watched his tall, lean form make its way behind Rocky's counter, where she gave him a quick squeeze before he slipped through the swinging door. I imagined him sitting on the one chair in the small kitchen, and I lifted up a hope of a bit of peace and quiet for him there.

As he made his way out of the shop, Galen stopped by where I was straightening the window around not just my two dogs but his, too, and said, "That was an interesting group." He raised an eyebrow but didn't say anything further. "We'll see you tomorrow night." He snapped, and Mac followed him out the door.

I watched them make their way to Galen's smart car and smiled. The two of them were quite a pair, and I was grateful they'd been here today, both for their purchases and their calming presence. I'd have to catch them up on the events of the week soon.

Now, though, I needed to call about that second register and also double-check my tracking numbers for Harrow's extra books. Otherwise, tomorrow night was going to be a bit of a tangle of waiting and disappointment.

Fortunately, my supplier could overnight me another register that I could pay for over time with no interest, and the tracking information said my extra books were out for delivery. All was well.

When Marcus came back from his break, we spent a few minutes beefing up the front windows and tables, and he began to prep the space for the reading tomorrow by creating one of his now-classic displays for Harrow's books. This time, he used a table, some doubled-over cardboard, and a lot of packing tape to craft a large tower by the stage. When he added the silhouettes of three female figures to the base, I grinned. It looked just like it came from Harrow's second book, and I knew she would love it – as would our customers.

As if he knew we were ready, the delivery man wheeled in two hand trucks full of book boxes and dropped them, at Marcus's direction, right by the display. Then, we filled the tower with titles in stacks and face-outs that complemented Marcus's design and displayed the books to their full glory.

With a few more titles, we added to the front windows, and then Marcus carefully arranged the extra copies behind the register so that we could easily fill in with them or sell them off as needed. If we moved all this inventory today and tomorrow, we'd beat our sales records by a long shot, and if the number of people who were still coming by to enter to win seats to the event tomorrow were any indication, we were going to smash our previous records into powder.

At noon, I headed toward the front door for my lunch break and was met by the sheriff, who gave me a quick hug and said, "Let's get some tacos."

I could eat his wife Lu's tacos for three meals a day seven

days a week, so he didn't have to ask twice. But given how drawn his face was, I offered to get our food and bring it back so that he could have a minute to sit and rest.

"That's kind, Harvey, but I'd like to get out into the sunshine a bit, find a quiet place to talk." He gave me a pointed look that I understood immediately. Too many ears here.

I caught Stephen's eye as I headed out the door before Tuck, and when he nodded, I knew he got the message. He needed to stay alert and let me know if I was needed. Marcus had the store well in hand, but given the threats this week, I didn't want Marcus and Rocky alone in the store, not with Dooley and his racist friends wandering around so brazenly.

I tried to put the store out of my mind for a few minutes as we walked up the street to Lu's truck and asked Tuck how he was doing. "Just a couple of weeks, right?"

He nodded. "Not even. Just twelve days." He glanced back at me. "Thanks for all the ways you've supported me, Harvey. I really appreciate it."

I stepped up and slipped my arm through his. "That's what friends do, Tucker Mason. You'd do the same for me."

He leaned back at bit and looked down at me. "You're not thinking of running for office are you?"

I laughed so hard my lungs hurt. "No, don't worry. I'm quite content to be a business owner in town."

We chatted the rest of the way to Lu's truck and then along the path to the river through town, and by the time we came to sit down, I had almost forgotten we were in the midst of a crisis. Almost.

7

W hile we ate our first taco, I tried to savor the moment of quiet with the rippling water below and the covered bridge just to my right, but the longer Tuck stayed silent, the more anxious I became until finally I said, "Okay, what do I need to know?" My voice was a bit shriller than I'd expected, and Tuck actually winced.

"You okay?" he asked. "I mean, considering."

I sighed. "Sometimes. But just now, I'm eager for you to tell me what you want to tell me so I can stop imagining the worst."

Tuck studied me for a minute. "That brain of yours, Harvey. It's a gift and curse, huh?"

"You said it." I took a deep breath and then looked at my friend again.

"Okay, so here's the thing. Roger Birmingham is, indeed, Catherine's foster father. For the most part, social services had only good things to say about him," Tuck said.

I squinted. "For the most part."

"There's that brain going into productive action." He grinned at me. "So I finally got a hold of Catherine's last case worker. She'd left social services and was a bit hard to track down, but when I did, boy did she paint a different picture of things."

"How so?" I asked as I took a bite of my second taco. It was a good sign if I still wanted to eat.

"She didn't have anything directly bad to say about Roger or his wife. She said they seemed to take good care of Catherine, no signs of abuse or neglect, and they attended her events at school and such." He looked out across the water.

"But?" I asked between bites.

"But she and Catherine got close, and Catherine told her that the Birminghams had finally caved and told her about how awful her birth parents were, about how they were addicts and dealers and how they had left Catherine alone for days while they went after their next fix." The crease between Tuck's eyebrow deepened.

"That sounds a lot like what Hugo and Horatio told me," I said as I wiped my mouth with my napkin and studied my friend. "Why does that bother you?"

"Because I can't find any criminal records at all for Catherine's birth parents, Cato and Delia Edwards." He turned to look at me, "And neither could Catherine's final case worker."

"That does seem odd, but maybe they were just never charged with a crime," I said.

Tuck shrugged. "Maybe, but when the case worker began digging, a lot of things turned out to be a bit shady."

"Shady how?" I said as the pit grew larger and larger in my stomach.

"Well, there's the lack of criminal record for her parents, but also, the case worker couldn't find any intake paperwork on Catherine at all. It's like one day she just appeared as a foster child to the Birminghams with no paper trail." Tuck took a huge bite of his carnitas taco and looked at me, waiting.

I took a deep breath. "So are you saying that the Birminghams kidnapped her?" My mind was flying as I tried to tie what

Tuck was saying with something that felt familiar, and then I had it – I'd just read a book about a story like this, *The Moonlight Child*.

Tuck sighed. "I don't know. It's possible that there was something up with Catherine's biological parents and they asked the Birminghams to take care of her." He turned back toward the river. "But I doubt it."

The pit that had settled somewhere below my diaphragm climbed into my throat. "So all that stuff about their being addicts, all the stuff that Catherine believed about her genetics and her predisposition to addiction . . ." I felt like crying.

"Likely all lies told so she wouldn't go looking for her parents," Tuck said.

His words sparked a memory from earlier in the week. "But Roger and the Hardware Brothers both said that she did go looking and that she found them. That it was that meeting that sent her spiraling." I looked at Tuck. "But they thought it was because her parents were addicts."

"And if they weren't, but you had believed your whole life that they were . . ." Tuck said quietly.

"It might send me right into the thing I had worked so hard to avoid my whole life," I whispered.

"Exactly," Tuck said.

We both sat and watched the water flow by for a while. Somehow, this news made Catherine's death even more tragic. If she'd been lied to her whole life, if she had believed something completely wrong about her parents, if she'd actually been the victim of the Birminghams instead of the beloved child she thought she was . . . the thought brought tears to my eyes.

Then, I gasped. "Oh no, do Jared and Symeon know all this?" I asked as my heart began to race.

"They do. I sent Jared a text from Lu's phone this morning as soon as I had my suspicions. He'll suss out what the truth is."

Tuck turned and looked at me. "He's very good at his job, Harvey. He's safe."

I wanted to believe my friend. I wanted to trust my boyfriend, but just then, my nervous system was telling me that Jared and Symeon were in grave danger. "Thoughts aren't things," I whispered.

Tuck put his arm around me and pulled me close. I wasn't sure if he was comforting me or himself, but I didn't care.

I WAS grateful for Tuck's presence as we walked back to the store, but I didn't know what to say. At this point, my anxiety was so high that I couldn't think about anything but Jared. But of course, thinking about Jared was only making my anxiety higher. Fortunately, the store was swamped with customers when we walked in, and I immediately went into bookstore owner mode, a state of being that bypassed the part of my brain that was making me terrified and calmed me down so I could sell and recommend books.

Tuck took a seat in the café with a coffee and his latest read, *Remains of the Day*, and each time I passed, he looked up, nodded, and smiled. Clearly, he had a mission to keep me calm by being here, and I couldn't say I hated it. After all, if Jared needed help, he'd call Tuck, and if Tuck sped out of here, I'd know something was wrong.

What I'd do with that knowledge I couldn't have begun to say, but still, I was grateful to feel like I might know something if there was something to know.

APPARENTLY WALTER and Stephen had packed up their fundraising efforts while we were gone, and while I was sad to not have been able to say goodbye, I couldn't say I thought I could handle remembering to send people their way that afternoon. I made a note in my phone to check in with them about how everything had gone.

But between the need to continually restock the Harrow books, answer the phone about questions for the Harrow event, and ring up customers buying Harrow's books, I was pretty well preoccupied. So much so, in fact, that when Jared and Symeon came in the back door about three, I didn't even bat an eye.

At least at first, but then I stared at them as they stood near the back wall and wondered what to do. When Jared started toward me, I forced my feet to drag me forward and went to him. But then I stopped, worried that someone like Dooley or Birmingham might see. Jared didn't stop though, and in a moment, he had wrapped me in a tight hug. "It's done, Harvey. We're safe, and we aren't going back."

I slumped against him with relief and barely held back my tears. Then I stepped back and said, "Why? What happened?"

"They got what we needed," Tuck said as he joined us. "Great work guys."

I stared from man to man and then I blurted, "Does Mart know?"

The bell over the door jingled, and my best friend barged in.

"She does," Symeon said as he caught Mart mid-flight. "I texted her as soon as we got in the car."

She kissed her boyfriend firmly and then, when he finally set her down, she said, "Okay, so we need details."

I nodded vigorously and started to head toward the café. But then the bell over the door rang, and when I instinctively looked to see who was coming in, I saw it was Alix Harrow herself and stopped dead.

"Holy crap," I whispered far too loudly. "That's Alix Harrow." I turned to Jared with wide eyes. "I think I have to go talk to her."

"Of course you do," he said as he squeezed my hand. "It's

not a good idea to debrief here anyway. My house. Seven o'clock." He kissed my cheek, and then he and Tuck walked out the front door with a lilt in their steps.

I, however, had lead feet once again, and it was only when Marcus slipped his arm through mine and pulled me closer to our guest that my brain kicked back into gear. "Ms. Harrow," I said as I extended my hand. "I'm Harvey Beckett, the owner here. It's so nice to see you, but I'm afraid to say we weren't expected you until tomorrow."

"Exactly. I decided to take a little Mom's night out here in your gorgeous town, so I'm just browsing and hanging out. I was actually hoping you wouldn't recognize me." She said with a smile.

I blushed. "Oh no, I'm so sorry to bother you then."

"No, no, I didn't mean it that way. Sorry," she said with a wave of her hand. "I just don't want you to fuss. I really am here just to shop, but if you could recommend a quiet place for an early dinner, I would be grateful."

I told her about Chez Cuisine up the street and then waved Symeon over from where he and Mart were talking by the café. "This is their head chef, Symeon. I expect he can whip up something you'd love."

Symeon put out his hand. "Be happy to, Ms. Harrow." I shot Mart a look of gratitude for filling him in about our special guest. "We do French food with a rustic twist. I'll keep an eye out for you when you come over." He smiled and headed toward the door.

Harrow smiled. "Sounds perfect. See you in a bit."

Marcus stepped forward and introduced himself. "Can I help you find anything in particular?" he said. Somehow, he made his question sound perfectly pitched, like he was willing to help but that he also knew she knew her books.

"Actually, if you could just point me in the direction of the memoirs, I'd be grateful," she answered.

"Right this way," Marcus said as he walked her around the shelves to our now-larger memoir section and then came right back.

"Oh my goodness," I whisper-squealed.

Marcus nodded. "I know. She's here, and she's shopping."

I was definitely Harrow's number one fan in St. Marin's, but Marcus was a very close second. "I'm going to check the window and the display, just in case she walks around," he said as he darted toward the front of the store.

I stood frozen in the middle of the floor for a second until Mart came over and said, "Latte time?"

I sighed. "Definitely. This day has, I think, gotten the best of me." Suddenly, I was exhausted, but I had several more hours of work and then dinner to stay awake for. Caffeine was absolutely necessary.

Either Rocky had seen us and knew what we needed or Mart had pre-ordered because by the time we reached the counter, our drinks were ready. Two huge vanilla lattes with a chocolate scone and two forks. "You guys need to pamper yourselves a bit. Best girlfriends ever."

I chuckled. "If that's the case, then you need to join us."

"Already ahead of you," Rocky said as she pulled her own mug from behind the espresso machine. "Mind if I sit, too?"

"Please," Mart said and led us to a window-side table so we could people watch while she sipped. "So did Jared tell you anything?"

I dropped into my chair and shook my head. "Said it wasn't the place. Tonight, I guess." I hadn't realized I was a little annoyed by the lack of information until that moment, but I definitely was. "Nothing from Symeon either?"

Mart shook her head and frowned. "I got the same spiel."

Rocky studied me and then Mart. "Women, you realize these guys are protecting you, right? They don't want you to be worried all afternoon. They're safe, and they know that's what you needed to know most. Go easy on them. You think *you've* had a hard day?" Her tone was playful, but I could hear the force in her words.

I set my mug down and sighed. "You're right. My curiosity is just killing me." I rolled my shoulders back, "But not as much as having Jared undercover. Gracious that was grueling."

"Imagine how they felt." Mart said.

I realized, with a jolt, that I hadn't really thought about how Jared was feeling all day. I was so caught up in my own anxiety that it had blotted out any sense of compassion I had. I needed to get that under control because it made me a version of myself that I didn't like very much. "They must have been terrified."

Rocky sighed. "I expect so, but at least they found something out." She looked at Mart. "Symeon doesn't have to work tonight?"

Mart smiled. "Max asked if he could come in and set up, get the sous-chef started, prep Harrow's dinner, and then suggested he have the night off." Mart turned to me. "Clearly, I'm glad you aren't dating Max, but he really isn't a bad guy, huh?"

"Not as bad as he wants everyone to think he is," I said with a laugh. "That girlfriend of his seems to be bringing out the best in him."

"Girlfriends do that," Rocky said, and we all grinned at our own goodness.

I WAS SO ABSORBED in our silly banter that I didn't even notice Alix Harrow walking our way until she said hi to all of us. "Sorry to bother you, Harvey, but Marcus tells me you have a tattoo."

I blushed so hard that I felt like all the blood in my body was in my cheeks. "I do," I said and slid the sleeve on my sweater up to show her the script on the inside of my left fore-arm. "Your book changed me."

She took my hand in hers and studied the word etched into my skin. "wordworker."

"I am so honored. Do you mind if I take a picture for my Instagram?" she asked as she held up her phone. "I'll tag the store for sure."

My blush deepened, which I didn't know was possible, but I nodded. "Of course." I slid my bracelet down my arm and held the tattoo facing her with the bookstore in the background. When she showed me the pic a few seconds later, I was delighted to see the store looked wonderful and the tattoo crisp.

"Thank you so much, Harvey." She slipped her phone into her pocket and slid the All Booked Up tote bag back to her hand. "I'll be here at eleven tomorrow to pre-sign if that's okay."

"Of course, and if you don't have plans, maybe we could get lunch. We have the best Mexican food truck around," I said.

"Sounds good. They do have mole, right?" she asked as she headed for the door.

"Best I've ever had," I said with a smile.

When she'd gone out the door and passed us with a wave from the sidewalk, I collapsed onto the table. "Alix Harrow just took a picture of my tattoo and agreed to have lunch with me tomorrow. I can die now," I whispered.

"Oh, somehow, I think a certain sexy police officer might disagree with that statement," Rocky said as she stood and pushed in her chair. "Come to think of it, I'd disagree, too."

"Me, three," Mart added.

Mart followed me into the store and said, "Okay, what do we need to do to get ready for tomorrow?"

I glanced at my phone to check the time. "Well, we could get the chairs out," I said with a look toward the stage, where Marcus was refilling Harrow's display yet again.

"Great. A little lifting will get my blood flowing and help me shake off the last of my nerves." She headed toward the back room and returned a moment later with a rolling cart full of chairs that she began to arrange in front of the stage.

Marcus smiled over at me and then jogged to the register where I was standing with the last of my latte. "Good idea," he said before he studied my face. "Did you let her take a picture?"

"You are in so much trouble, Marcus Dawson," I said with a wag of my finger. "I can't believe you did that."

"Are you serious? She was thrilled. Imagine that someone loved something you created enough to have it permanently applied to their body. You honored her work, Harvey." Marcus squeezed my arm and headed to the back.

I hadn't thought of it like that, but I guessed he was right. As I watched him wheel another cart of chairs out, I took a deep breath and decided to be happy that today was ending in such a spectacular way. Jared and Symeon were safe. They'd gotten good information, apparently, and Alix Harrow had liked my tattoo enough to share it on her Insta. Wow, who would have thought it?

THE REST of the afternoon flew by. Harrow had indeed gone to Max's restaurant, where Symeon had made her a duck confit, on a bed of mushroom risotto with a side of mixed greens. Apparently, she'd loved it, so said his texts to Mart, and she'd mentioned Chez Cuisine on her Instagram stories, right after the link to my shop's feed with the picture of my tattoo. I had to hold back a squeal when I looked on my phone.

We had a steady stream of customers, and both Marcus and I recommended titles, rang up sales, and answered questions by phone and in person about Harrow's reading. At six, when it was time for me to draw the winning seats and call the lucky people, Mart took a video of my drawing – "for TikTok but also for credibility" – and when I called the lucky young women who had won, both of them had sounded like they were about to cry. Harrow had a lot of die-hard fans.

By the time we finished tidying up the store, refilling all the displays, and cashing out the register, it was right at seven, and Marcus, Mart, and I took it upon ourselves to ask the lingering customers to head out because, as they knew, we had a big day ahead. Everyone quickly packed up, made their last purchases, and headed out with a discount card for Rocky's café, and we closed up the store and made our way around the corner to Jared's house.

I'd been so busy with customers and Alix Freakin' Harrow that I hadn't thought much about dinner in any way, but now, I was absolutely famished. So when the smell of grilling meat hit me at the walkway to Jared's house, my knees wanted to buckle a bit. It might have been chicken or sausage, steak even – I didn't care. I was just so eager to see my boyfriend and eat what he was cooking that I almost sprinted around to the back of the house, my friends close behind.

I stopped short as I rounded the corner into the backyard because it was full of my friends. Everyone was there – Cate and Lucas, Bear and Henri, Pickle, Stephen and Walter, Woody, Tuck and Lu, Elle, and even Symeon, already off the clock from the restaurant. When I noticed that they all had drinks, I beelined toward the silver bucket full of hard lemonade that I spied near the base of Jared's back steps and tried to be cool by slamming the bottle open on the side of the porch railing.

As usual, my attempts to be cool resulted in no coolness and a big bruise, but fortunately, Jared stepped over with both a bottle opener and a towel full of ice and soothed my ego and my sore hand. "That's a thing, right?" I asked him as he led me to a chair near the grill and then turned back to the chicken breasts that were cooking on a steady blaze of charcoal.

"It's definitely a thing, but it takes just the right angle and a good wallop of your hand at just the right spot."

I sighed. "At least I got the walloping part right," I said. "So you invited everyone?"

"Tuck's idea. He thought it was probably best to just catch everybody up at once, and there's also something he needs our help with."

"Sounds good." I stood up as I took a long pull from my bottle. "Now, how can I help you?"

He leaned over and kissed me quickly. "Nothing. You just relax. I have all the help I need."

As if on cue, my parents walked around from the back of Jared's house with platters full of food – rice pilaf, green beans, some sort of macaroni salad. "You asked my parents to help?" I asked as I tried to process what was happening.

"*Asked* might not be the right word. *Acquiesced* perhaps." He winked at me as Mom zipped by and gave me a wink. "They've been really great."

I stared at him a second. "How many questions have you answered, and did my father make you sit under a bare lightbulb?"

"A million. And no . . . but I did wonder why the lampshade was off on the light over the sink." He smiled at me. "It's been fine. They are kind of a force, but a gentle one. And besides, I want to get to know them more."

I blushed. "Well, thanks. But let me know if they get to be too much. They can be, well, a lot."

"You remember I know their daughter pretty well, right?" He grinned and planted another kiss on my cheek.

"What exactly are you saying?" I asked with a broad smile.

Mart and Symeon came over and joined us, pulling two camping chairs behind them. "So when do we get to know the scoop?" Mart asked.

"As soon as everyone has food," Jared answered as he

handed Symeon a platter to hold while he pulled the chicken off the grill. "Which should be in just a few minutes now. Patience, young one," he said as he patted Mart on the shoulder before carrying the chicken to the table.

"Please, everyone come eat," Jared shouted over the din of conversation. "Before it gets cold."

One thing I loved about my friends is that they were not at all shy about food, and Cate was up and in line before Jared even moved away from the table. Pickle and then Henri followed suit, and soon everyone was lined up waiting to chow down.

I made my way to the end of the line, confident that I'd get some of that delicious-smelling chicken but also feeling a little bit too over-peopled to chat while we waited. Fortunately, Jared sidled up and just let me lean on him as we waddled our way up the line. I filled my plate so full that I didn't even have room for a cupcake, but Jared made up for my lack of planning by scoring a second plate and grabbing three cupcakes, one chocolate, one vanilla, and one lemon, for us to share. Or so he thought.

We pulled our chairs out away from the grill and joined in the circle that seemed to so naturally form when all of us were together. Then, I tucked into the food and discovered that Jared was, indeed, the best grill cook I'd ever met. The meat was smoky and tangy, and the herbs he'd use for the sauce were just perfect. I normally wasn't the biggest fan of chicken, but I could eat this every night.

Between that, the amazing almond green beans Mom had made, the macaroni salad with feta, and the two pieces of French bread that I slathered in butter, I was plenty full by the time Tuck cleared his throat to get our attention. I put my plate down and shifted the cupcakes into my lap. Jared grinned at me and quickly got up to get his own dessert. He knew me well.

Then, as Tuck began to explain what Symeon and Jared

had uncovered that day, I slowly devoured the icing off the lemon cupcake as I listened. It was good to have something else to focus on as I realized that what Tuck was sharing was more on the standards of a major conspiracy theory and less like a bunch of doofuses in pickups.

"First and foremost, you all need to know that Bryan Dooley and the men who work with him on his campaign are verified members of Identity Dixie, a recognized hate group that focuses on white supremacy and male domination." Tuck's voice was serious and dead even, as it always was when he talked about his work.

I scanned the circle of my friends, and for the most part, they didn't seem surprised, although Henri's dark skin had reddened considerably in the last few moments. A sure sign she was livid.

"Secondly, they are actively recruiting new members under the guise of Dooley's campaign. Jared, could you explain more?" Tuck asked as he sat down.

Jared swallowed the bite of chocolate cupcake he had just taken and stood up. "Thanks to Symeon's expert ability to play the bigot, we were both invited to formally join ID, as they regularly call their organization. We were then asked to invite other 'appropriate' men to join us as we visited homes to talk about the election and gather confirmation that folks would be voting for Dooley."

"Did you use voting rosters to know that?" Lucas asked.

"Right. We had the Board of Elections lists, just as any candidate could, and we visited anyone whose voting history appeared to align with Dooley's positions," Jared answered.

"So if they'd voted for bigots in the past?" Elle said.

"Yes, but also if they voted for anti-immigration candidates or anyone who wanted to end affirmative action. Basically, if they had shown they wanted to support a system that favored white men—" Symeon added.

"White straight cis men," Walter corrected."

"White straight cis men, yes. Thanks, Walter," Symeon said. "Then we talked to them. It was horrible."

"What do you mean?" Mart asked.

Symeon pulled his hand down over his face. "I guess I really thought most of those folks who flew the Confederate flag or talked about ending welfare were well-intentioned – maybe ill-informed – but truly trying to do the right thing. But today, I learned, once a bunch of us talked to them, that they really just wanted what they wanted for people who looked and lived like them. It was all about getting their own way, no matter whose backs they had to step on."

I sighed and applauded Symeon's willingness to be honest, even as I felt a little weary that it had taken him this long to see the reality of the world. As a woman, I'd long known that the patriarchy and many men in it would talk the good talk about women's rights as long as it didn't cost them anything, and from what I'd learned from my LGBTQ friends and my friends of color, it was exactly the same, or maybe worse, when it came to ethnicity, culture, and sexual and gender orientation.

Before I let myself be too hard on Symeon though, I remembered how much people had put up with my nonsense when I hadn't yet learned to see my own privilege as a white, straight, cis, middle-class woman. And I knew it was even harder for white, straight, cis, middle-class men because they were, metaphorically and literally speaking, at the top of the privilege pyramid. The world actually worked as we all thought it should for them, and to step into a place where you took on some of what made the world hard for other people was a challenge, even for good-intentioned people.

Henri looked at Symeon intently. "Welcome to the real world, honey. It's good to have you join us." There was no venom in her words, only honesty and a touch of weariness.

Symeon gave her a small smile and then said, "It's good to be here, and I'm really sorry it took me so long to arrive."

Mart reached over and wrapped both of her arms around one of his. "But you have arrived, and now we can do something." She looked over at Jared. "What are we going to do?"

"There's not much we can do about their campaigning, honestly. As far as I could tell, they were well within the bounds of the law," Jared paused. "But in terms of the threats against Tuck, that's another story."

"They admitted that?" Pickle asked, his attorney's ears perking up.

"Sort of," Symeon sighed. "Roger Birmingham said that one of their goals was to get Tuck to drop out of the race."

Pickled looked interested. "Okay, but that's not the same as threatening him."

"No, it's not," Jared added, "but when they asked us where Tuck lived and if we'd be willing to help with a little intimidation, they crossed a line."

The gasp that passed around the circle was audible and intense. "They wanted you to threaten Tuck?" I hissed.

"Not him directly, but they did want us to tear up his house a bit. 'Just to scare him,'" Symeon said as he made air quotes.

"You have that recorded?" Pickle asked.

"Yep. Already sent the file to the district attorney. I expect we'll be making a couple of arrests tomorrow," Tuck said.

"After that we bailed," Symeon said.

"You just walked out?" Bear asked.

"Yeah, we both said that we didn't want to face jail time for something so minor and that we wouldn't be a part of that," Jared said. "As best I could tell, they believed us. They called us a few choice names that involved parts of the female anatomy and told us not to bother turning in our membership paperwork."

I was so glad both Jared and Symeon were out of that mess,

but the way these men were threatening Tuck made my blood boil. "So arrests of?" I let the question hang in the air.

"Dooley is smart," Jared said. "He made sure he wasn't there when Birmingham and the other guys asked us to vandalize Tuck's house, so we can't arrest him. But Birmingham and the other two men, they'll be facing charges."

I nodded and tried to feel happy about that. "Did you find out anything about Catherine's murder?" I felt bad asking since clearly the guys were happy about this result.

Jared's face instantly clouded over. "Not yet, but Birmingham did tell me a fair bit about her, about her biological parents and their supposed drug problems."

"But we know that wasn't true, or at least probably not true," I said as I looked from Jared to Tuck.

"Right," Tuck said and then caught the rest of our friends up on what he'd told me earlier about the strange anomalies in Catherine's foster care story.

"That poor girl," Cate said. "She was set up for a crisis."

"It's a tragedy of major proportions," Jared said, "and Roger Birmingham thinks that he and his wife, Kara, is her name, did the right thing by that young woman."

I sighed. "Any sense he killed her?"

Symeon shook his head. "I don't think so. He was really torn up about her death, even cried a little. He is livid with Hugo and Horatio, though. He thinks they killed her."

I looked over at Tuck, who was looking up at the sky. "Is that possible?" I asked.

Tuck flipped his head down and met my eyes. "Maybe," he said quietly. "I wouldn't have thought so, but maybe."

"Why would they do that? What did they have to gain?" Lu asked her husband.

He sighed. "Apparently, Catherine stole from them. A lot."

I looked over at Jared and then Symeon, and they both

nodded. "When she was a kid?" I asked. "Surely the brothers aren't still upset about that."

"No, they aren't," Jared said. "She did steal some cash from them when she worked there as a teenager, but this theft was much more recent and much bigger."

When Jared paused, I sat forward and looked from one man to the other. "You can't tell us what she stole?" I asked as I tried to keep the exasperation out of my voice. They were already telling us much more than we technically needed to know, and my mind knew that. But my heart, which had been tested to its breaking today by events good and terrifying, was running the show now.

Jared looked over at Tuck, who gave a single nod. "Go ahead."

"She stole everything they had," Jared said.

8

After everyone else left, I stayed behind to help Jared clean up. Symeon and Mart had offered to stay, too, as had Mom and Dad, but I'd told them we had it in hand. We did, but mostly I just wanted time alone with my boyfriend. I needed it.

After Jared had dropped the bombshell about how Catherine had cleaned out all of Hugo and Horatio's bank accounts using the information she had about them from when she worked for them, the gathering had gone very still. All of us knew Hugo and Horatio, and as far as I knew, we all liked them, too. But it was hard not to imagine their anger when they found out Catherine had stolen all their hard-won earnings.

The brothers were close to retirement age, too, so they didn't have time to build up cash reserves again. The hardware store and inventory were probably worth a pretty penny, but not enough for the two of them to live on for the rest of their lives, especially if they wanted to do more than simply survive day to day.

As I dried the dishes that Jared washed – we'd decided to handwash as a way to unwind and talk with the gift of a little distraction that we both needed – I asked, "So how did she do it?"

Jared shook his head. "Like most of the people here in St. Marin's, Hugo and Horatio have had the same bank accounts for decades. And back in the day, they'd let Catherine help with the banking – making deposits, withdrawing cash for the register, that kind of thing."

I groaned. "So she still had all that information and used it."

"Exactly. All their accounts were linked, so she simply transferred everything to one account and then had a wire send all those funds to her own bank in the Caymans." Jared handed me a platter to dry.

"People actually have bank accounts in the Caymans?" I said. "I thought that was a TV thing."

"Nope, real thing. And while they will get their money back eventually, it's a whole lot easier to do that when the person who stole it is dead and didn't leave a will." Jared washed the last pot and handed it to me.

"Oh," I whispered, "so the brothers really did have motive." I hated that fact.

"Yeah, but so did Roger Birmingham, right? She had discovered that he had been lying to her all along, that her biological parents were good people who missed her, who didn't neglect her." Jared shook his head as he let the water drain out of the sink. "He was in trouble."

I nodded as I slid the pot back onto the rack above Jared's island and then sat down on a stool. "What about his wife? I mean wasn't she part of all this."

He sat down on the stool next to me. "Symeon tried really hard to get him to talk about his wife, but beyond saying she was 'a gem,' he wouldn't say much at all."

"Is that weird? It feels weird, but maybe I'm reading weird into things because this whole situation is so messed up." I stood up, went to Jared's cabinet, got two wine glasses, and opened the bottle of white wine from his fridge.

Jared poured us each a glass and then tipped his glass to ring against mine. "Cheers." He took a sip. "I can't decide if it's weird. Men don't always talk about things the way some women do. Like does your dad brag about your mom?"

I tried to think of times I'd heard my dad talk about my mom in public, and aside from answering questions about how she was, I couldn't think of a single instance when Dad had said much at all about Mom in public. He adored her, and he told me all the time about the things she did to make their lives better. But I couldn't recall one moment where he'd said something like that in public. "I guess not," I conceded. "Still, where is she? Why isn't she here?"

"Now, that I agree is very weird. If you were missing and your dad was going to look for you, wouldn't your mom insist on coming along?"

"Insist? She'd book the flights, rent the car, and find the hotel. There's no way she'd stay home." I paused and thought about that book I'd read about the kidnapped child. "What if she didn't know that Catherine was taken from good parents?"

Jared shook his head. "We still don't know the full story on Catherine's biological parents. It's possible they weren't so great, but it does seem very likely that things weren't on the up and up with the Birmingham foster care situation." He took a long swig of his wine. "But your point is valid. Maybe she was in the dark and her husband wanted to keep her that way."

I was starting to get an itch to start a murder board with our suspects and such, but I'd learned my lesson about getting that involved in a case. It never ended well for me or the people I loved. So I drank more wine and asked a question. "Any other suspects?"

Jared winked at me. "You really can't help yourself, can you?"

"Definitely not." I smiled. "But if you can't tell me, then don't. I don't want to make things harder for you or for Tuck."

He leaned over and kissed me lightly. "I can tell you, but this bit of information stays between us. Not even Mart, okay?"

I nodded and wondered if this is what Lu felt like when Tuck confided in her. "Okay."

"Bryan Dooley is our other suspect," he said

"Oh, wow. Okay." I couldn't decide if I was confused, thrilled, or angry and decided I was a little of both. "Explain?"

"Well, from what we could see today, Birmingham is Dooley's right-hand man in ID. He's not the face of the campaign – Dooley has a buttoned-up boy to run his campaign – but the real work of hate, that seems to be Roger's domain." Jared took a sip of wine and let me process this information.

I took a sip from my own glass and tried to make sense of all of this information. "So if Roger was caught out for kidnapping, then Dooley would be implicated in some sense? Am I understanding correctly?"

"Exactly," Jared said. "If it came out that one of the higher ups in Dooley's squad was a kidnapper, then Dooley's campaign would be jeopardized, and from what I can tell, he would do almost anything to win this election."

I tried to stop myself, but I let out a small giggle.

Jared stared at me. "What's so funny?"

"Sorry, I was picturing Dooley's squad like those squads on all the teenage shows where there's one cool kid, one nerd, one bully, one jock, and one pretty girl." I felt the laughter bubbling up again.

Jared smiled. "And who would Roger Birmingham be?"

I got suddenly serious. "Oh, that's easy. The bully."

"I thought you found him charming and sincere," Jared said.

"I did, which is why he's all the more dangerous. Bullies aren't just lugs who push and badger, you know? They can be real charmers who pull people close only to mow them down." I'd met a few of those people in my life before, and I'd just as soon never run into another of them again."

Jared pulled me into his chest and said, "I hear you." He stood back, took my hand, and led me to the couch.

"So what's next?" I asked as I snuggled against him. "What are you and Tuck going to do?"

He tugged me in tighter. "Why don't you let us worry about that, and you concentrate on the fact that you get to spend most of the day tomorrow with your favorite author?"

Some part of my brain buzzed with excitement, but the part of it that had been overtaxed that day dominated, and I mumbled an "mmm" before I let myself doze off against the firm chest beneath me.

WHEN I WOKE up the next morning, I woke up in Jared's bed, alone. I was still in my clothes from the day before, and I could smell coffee and sausage cooking below. I sat up and looked around Jared's room. It was tidy and warm, and the smell of his aftershave lingered amongst the wood furniture.

I let myself settle back down under the comforter and enjoy how comfortable I felt for a few minutes. More and more, I found myself imagining what life would look like if I lived here . . . with Jared. We hadn't been together that long, but at our age, we both knew what we wanted in a partner. I thought I'd found it in him, and I suspected he felt the same.

But that line of thinking wasn't going to get me anywhere today, not when I had a best-selling author to greet. I pivoted my feet to the ground and smiled when I saw a thick, blue robe draped over the chair. It felt a little silly to wear a robe over my clothes, but I did it anyway and reveled in the coziness as I walked down the stairs to Jared's kitchen.

I laughed out loud when I saw Taco and Mayhem settled on

either side of Jared's feet at the range. Both of them had their back legs splayed out behind them, and if I wasn't mistaken, I saw a little sausage grease on their chins, too. My pups were getting spoiled, big time.

"I see you have a couple of assistants," I said as I headed for the coffee pot beyond Jared, running a hand along his shoulders as I went.

"Official taste testers, thank you very much," he said. "How did you sleep?"

I thought a second, then said, "Well, since I can't remember sleeping, I think that must be a good sign, right?"

"I'd say. You didn't even stir when I carried you upstairs," he said with a shy grin.

I laughed. "Did that count as your workout yesterday?" I couldn't imagine carrying another grown adult anywhere, much less up a flight of stairs.

Jared tapped his fitness watch. "Bonus points. She thought it was interval training."

"She's gendered, then?"

"She is. Until you, she was my closest companion." He grinned.

I took my full mug and stepped up close behind him. "And now?"

"She pales in comparison," he said as he reached behind his back to hug me closer. "Absolutely pales."

I blushed as I kissed the space between his shoulder blades and then went to take a seat across from him. "So big plans for the day?"

"Some, but mostly, I plan to help my lovely girlfriend with her big day, starting with a good breakfast and then a meandering walk to work, if that's okay with her."

I grinned. "I like this plan." I paused and looked at him. "But you have other things to tend to today. I'll have lots of help."

"Oh, I know that. And if the troops hadn't already rallied, I would have rallied them." He picked up his phone from next to the range. "We've got our shifts planned.

I smiled and felt my heart thump. "You do? You've got first shirt, I take it?"

"First and third for lunch and then I'll be part of the team for this evening." He grinned then leaned over the counter to kiss me, almost burning his chest in sausage grease in the process.

"Careful there, sir. Don't mess up that fine physique," I said with a blush.

He grinned. "No way, not until you've seen it all," he said and blushed himself.

I waved a hand in front of my face. "Talk about distraction." I took out my own phone and texted Mart to see how her night was. I needed to think about something besides Jared's body.

"Mine was good. Quiet. And yours?" She included two winking emojis and one with its tongue out.

"It was great. Jared's bed is so comfortable," I teased.

Her response was the surprised emoji only.

"It was surprising since I slept in all my clothes. Now he's cooking for me," I replied.

"Good man, that one."

"Don't I know it. See you this afternoon?"

"Yep, my shift starts at three," she said.

"You all really do have this organized."

"Would you expect any less?" She signed off with two hearts, and I put my phone back in the robe pocket just as Jared plated up the sausage with biscuits he pulled hot from the oven. "Holy cow. It's like my own breakfast sandwich."

"Oh, it's not 'like' anything. It *is* your own breakfast sand-wich, à la Jared." He held out his hand and escorted me to the dining room, where he set the plate in front of me. "Enjoy."

"Aren't you coming to join me?" I asked with a bit of disappointment.

He came back in the room with the full coffee pot. "Of course, but first, caffeine."

AFTER JARED and I cleaned up from breakfast, we walked across town to my house so I could shower and change and then he took the dogs' leads as we made our way back into town and the shop just before nine.

Marcus and Rocky were already there, and I applauded when I saw the veritable tower of cinnamon rolls Rocky had on top of the pastry cabinet. "Your mom went all out," I said.

"Well, you've got her hooked on Harrow's books, so she wanted to show her appreciation to you and the author," Rocky said as she pointed to the tower. "Want one?"

I looked over at Jared beside me. "Later. Jared made me sausage and biscuits this morning, and I need a little time." I smiled at her. "But definitely later."

When I reached the door with Jared, I resisted the urge to plant a really long kiss on his lips and instead, pecked him on the cheek and said I looked forward to seeing him for our date with Alix Harrow.

He grinned and leaned forward. "I just look forward to seeing you see Alix Harrow," and then kissed me lightly.

I felt a little swimmy headed from all my time with Jared, but I knew the romance cobwebs would clear as I got to work. And since Marcus was way ahead of me on setting up the signing table for Harrow, I jumped right in and unloaded the rest of the books to the low crates beside her chair in the back room.

She would be doing signings for the reading tonight, too, but these copies were for anyone who couldn't come tonight but still wanted a signed edition. It was something I'd arranged with her publicist in advance after learning that popular authors always had more interest than we had space.

Once the signing space was set with a cup of water, a few pens in case she didn't bring her own, and a comfy cushion on the folding chair, Marcus and I headed back out to the floor to do a really good clean-up, with dustcloths and all.

Just before ten, the store was ready, the books were ready, and the cinnamon rolls were definitely ready. I headed over to grab mine, which Rocky heated briefly, and then took my position at the register with a fork in hand as Marcus let in the line of customers.

I smiled and greeted people as I subtly took bites of my cinnamon roll. I knew that some people would frown on eating at the counter this way, but I thought of it as advertising. Plus, I was long past the point of depriving myself to meet other people's standards.

Most everyone who had been waiting was milling around the books and café, and I was about done with my cinnamon roll and ready to give recommendations when I saw Walter and Stephen come in with their tablecloth and supplies. "You guys setting up again today?"

"If you don't mind," Walter said. "We had some good response yesterday, and we already passed our goal. So we thought we might double it today."

"I like your optimism! Of course, please do. I'll be in and out a bit more today. Harrow is arriving momentarily to sign, and then Jared and I are taking her to lunch," I smiled," but Marcus will be here all day if you need anything."

I gave the two men quick hugs just as I saw Harrow walk in the door. I tried to play it cool as I walked over, but really I felt the same way I did when one of the actors from a play I saw as a child signed my program. I could still remember his name, "Casey Gallagher." The program was in my mementos box.

But unlike six-year-old Harvey, I didn't jump up and down

as Harrow and I met for the second time. I simply extended my
hand, welcomed her, and asked if she would prefer to have a
coffee or a water while she signed.

"Any chance you can do a vanilla latte with a double shot?"
she asked. "I want to be fully on today."

"Absolutely," I said. "Want to browse while I put in your
order?"

She nodded and then walked further into the store, where
she stopped to talk with Walter and Stephen. I might have been
nervous that my friends would do a hard sell on the famous
author, but I knew these two well. Stephen and I had been
professional fundraisers together in California. He knew a hard
sell was never the right method, especially when someone
could make a big difference in an organization's financial
livelihood.

Rocky made up Harrow's drink when I reached the counter,
and she even made a broom-like image with the steamed milk.
"My compliments to the author," she said as she slid a
cinnamon roll onto a plate.

"I'll tell her," I said and walked back to where Harrow
waited. "This is for you, from our café owner, Rocky. Her
mother makes them."

"Well, that looks good enough to eat," she said as she took
the plate and the cup. "I will need fortifying for all these
signatures."

I smiled and led her to the back room, where she immediately sat down, sampled both the drink and the roll before
declaring them amazing, and went to signing.

For a few moments, I stood by and waited, wondering if I
could get her anything, but I quickly realized she had a
rhythm and process that didn't require even a second set of
hands. So I said, "Just shout if you need me. I'll be on the
floor."

"Perfect," she said. "These are ready if you want to put them out." She gestured toward a stack of all three of her titles. "I signed a few of each to get you started."

I grinned. "You've done this before."

"A few times," she said with a smile.

As I carried the books out to the display table by the register that Marcus had set up for the signed editions, he smiled. "She's fast."

I nodded and set the books down, but before I could even ask Marcus to arrange them, someone scooped up a copy of each and plopped them on the register. I looked up to see Henri smiling at me.

"What can I say? I'm a fan." She laughed.

I laughed my best sinister laugh and said, "Ah, my plan is working."

"It certainly is," Henri said as she handed me her card to pay.

I rang up her purchase with the standard friends and family discount and then handed over her books. "You're coming tonight, right?"

"Wouldn't miss it? And I'm on shift from two to four today, too. So see you in a bit. Enjoy lunch." She opened the book on the top of the stack and ran a finger over the signature as she grinned.

OVER THE COURSE of the next hour, Marcus and I stopped into the back room to check on Harrow and get the signed copies to add to our table. She was signing faster than we were selling, but not by much. I was very glad I'd ordered in almost double the copies because by tonight, I expected we'd be sold out.

Customers were steady that morning, and I spent a delightful few minutes with a teenage girl who wanted any books I could recommend on dragons. I immediately pulled *Eragon* off the shelf, and she studied the cover before deciding to buy the full series. Then, I asked if she was okay with non-YA titles, and she nodded. "My parents have given me permission to read whatever I want, as long as I talk to them about anything that bothers me."

"That sounds like a great family policy," I said and then walked her over to the fantasy section and grabbed the first book in Anne McCaffrey's Dragon Riders of Pern series. The customer scooped up that full series, too, and as I rang her out, she asked if she could sit and read a while.

"Of course, and I'll treat you to a café drink for investing so heavily in your new interest. What would you like?"

Having gotten her squared away with a vanilla steamer at Rocky's recommendation, I made my way back to Harrow to see how she was doing. My timing was perfect since she was just closing the final copy of *Splintered Spindle*.

"You probably need a hand massage after all of that." I said as I picked up the final stack of titles. "Hang out here as long as you'd like. We'll go to lunch in a few minutes if that still suits."

"Sounds perfect. I just need to meet Galen for my video before we go," she said as she stood and stretched.

I smiled and pointed her to the restroom before dropping off the final signed copies and looking for Galen, our erstwhile in-house Instagram and TikTok marketer. Not surprisingly, I found him in the mystery section, where he was making his usual stack of titles, including a paracozy called *Vanilla Bean Vampire*.

"Didn't think you were into the magical stuff," I said as I sidled up to him.

"Lately, I've been giving it a go and enjoying the idea that maybe the woman who bakes my bread actually imbues it with something special," he said with a wink.

"Like rye flour?" I joked.

"Exactly." He winked. "I'm going to do a little filming with your special guest if that's alright with you."

"She mentioned that, and of course it's okay. Then maybe you'll join us for lunch?"

"I'd love that as long as Mack can stay here with his buddies." He looked over at where the Bulldog had his head resting on Mayhem's rump. "I'd hate to disturb him."

"Of course not. We'll leave all of them here, and I'll give my two a good stroll when we get back."

Harrow walked up beside me. "I'm ready for my close-up," she said.

Galen extended his hand. "Wonderful. Ms. Harrow, I'm Galen. Thanks for agreeing to do this with me."

"I'm honored. I love your Insta stuff, and your TikTok videos are so smart." She leaned over and gave him a quick hug. "What's your plan?"

I left them to it as Galen started to talk about how he wanted to film her walking through the store, then with her books, and then leaving with a big stack of titles. I'd see enough of Galen's videos to know they'd include some great music and effects to be eye-catching without seeming gaudy.

For the next few minutes, I did my best to stay off camera while I tidied up the store and checked in with Stephen and Walter. Apparently, they'd had another great morning, and Harrow had just mentioned that she'd post a picture of them with a mention of Coming to the Table on her own social feeds. They were over the moon and eager to stay on for the afternoon. "If you don't mind?" Stephen asked.

"I love it, as long as you won't be too tired to come to the reading tonight," I said.

"We're on for the dinner shift, so we'll already be here. Our assignment, à la Jared, was to get dinner into the back room promptly at five." Walter winked at me.

"Well that answers one dilemma for me. What are we eating tonight?"

"We're going with finger foods; charcuterie, if you will,"

Stephen said with a horrible Italian accent. "And a little cider to help take the edge off."

I grinned. "That sounds perfect. Who else is on the dinner shift?"

"Everyone, technically. But mostly us for dinner and your parents and Jared for set-up," Walter answered. "We've all been instructed to be here by six at the latest to help prep the store, greet guests, staff the register, and support you."

"Maybe I'll just go home and take a nap then," I said with a tiny bit more longing than I intended.

"Actually," Jared said as he walked up behind me. "You're on schedule for that just after lunch. Then Marcus gets his break when you get back."

I turned and looked at him. "You've thought of everything." I gave him a quick peck on the lips and then saw Harrow and Galen heading toward us. "Ready?"

"Yep," they said in unison and then laughed.

"Bring you anything?" I asked Stephen and Walter.

"Actually, our lunch should be delivered any minute." Stephen looked at the front door. "Right on time."

Elle was walking in with three covered to-go containers from Max's. "Enjoy lunch. I've got the register, and the men here can eat."

I took a deep breath, made a forced effort to let all my nerves go, and then led the way out the door and up the street to where Lu was parked by the hardware store. Apparently, Jared had prepped her, too, because she had set up a folding table in a parking spot just ahead of her truck, and as we walked up, she brought out two platters full of her specialties. "I'll be right back with the extra mole," she said.

"Well, this is the first time I've eaten street food at a table on the street," Harrow said with a laugh. "I love it."

We chatted and ate as St. Mariners wandered by with a stare and a wave. In every way, we were the talk of the town, which was, I suspected, exactly what Jared and Lu had planned.

As we rested a few minutes to let the food settle before we tasted Lu's amazing flan, Harrow said, "I hope this isn't indelicate to ask, but the paper said someone was murdered here this week."

I nodded. "A young woman. Yes. A real tragedy."

"It is," Harrow said. "That must have been a shock in such a nice, quiet town."

Jared actually guffawed. "You'd be surprised at our murder rate, I bet." When Harrow frowned, "It's just a quirky statistic. St. Marin's is completely safe."

"Especially when you eat with the police," Galen added.

At that moment, a woman marched over from the sidewalk and stood looming above our table with her hands on her hips. She looked to be about sixty with florid skin and a wild mane of brown hair that looked like it had once been the result of an expensive cut. "Just what I figured. You're out here gossiping about Catherine. Of course."

I stared at the woman and shook my head slowly. "I'm sorry. Do we know you?"

"I'm Kara Birmingham, Catherine's mother." She huffed out a hard breath. "I came here thinking you all would be distraught over a death in your so-called adorable town, but here you are talking about her like she's the latest gossip, and with the police to boot." She poked a finger into Jared's shoulder.

Galen stood and extended his hand to Harrow. "May I escort you to your car?"

She rose and nodded. "I'd appreciate that. Thank you, Harvey and Jared. This has been lovely." Then she turned, took Galen's arm, and walked back up the street.

I watched them for a moment before turning to Ms. Birmingham. "Would you like to join us?"

She scowled at me. "Are you kidding? You want me to sit down and chat about my daughter's death like I'm the town crier. No, thank you." But she didn't walk away.

"Actually, I'd like to talk to you as part of the investigation," Jared said, "if you have time just now. I know there are a lot of things to be taken care of, but your help would be immeasurable." His voice had taken on an almost obsequious tone, and I had to turn away and fake a cough to keep from rolling my eyes.

Mrs. Birmingham looked from him to me and then back to him. "Okay, but not here. In a proper place like the police station."

"Of course," Jared said as he stood. "I'll see you later," he said to me with a wink that Mrs. Birmingham couldn't see.

I carried our dirty plates and the uneaten flan to Lu. "Would you mind if I took this to share with the folks at the store? They've been working hard."

"Of course," she said. "Who was that woman?"

"Catherine Birmingham's mother," I said quietly.

"Oh, well, then I won't give her a stern lecture about not making a scene," Lu said with a grimace.

"It was a moment," I said. "Jared is taking her to the station to talk."

" Should I let Tuck know?" she asked.

"I was thinking about that, too, but it might be better if Mrs. Birmingham doesn't think we all share information, no matter how true that might be."

Lu nodded. "Okay, I've got the rest of this. See you in a few hours." She waved me off, and I headed back to the shop to check in before walking the dogs. Galen had already retrieved Mack, which was good because given the excitement of my two, I didn't think I could manage three pups on a stroll.

Marcus assured me that he and Elle had things under control, so with a word of thanks, Mayhem, Taco, and I headed out toward home on a circuitous route. The plan was for them to get a good walk and then be left in the backyard until Mart came home about four. She'd feed them and then bring them to the store for tonight's activities.

The hounds would have been totally fine to be at the store for the full day, but I also knew that they might get restless during the reading if they weren't fed. This way, we all got a break, got our meals, and got to enjoy the time together tonight.

The autumn air was brisk, and I picked up our pace a bit to keep warm. I wasn't sure exactly what time Jared would make it to my house, or if he would, but I figured I'd probably benefit as much from a good walk as from a nap. So we made our way to the edge of town by the river's edge, where I let the dogs sniff.

I looped the pups' leashes around my ankle and sat down on a bench to stare at the water for a bit. I wasn't one of those people who adored the beach. It didn't hold much interest for me except when it was deserted in the winter. But the water – a river, a lake, a stream even – those things filled my spirit in a way I couldn't quite articulate. I was so grateful to live near the water so that on busy days when everything felt a little frantic, I could sit still and let the water do the running.

Mayhem and Taco busied themselves with all the scents they could reach in a two-foot radius around me and then settled at my feet in the sun to bask and sniff. I stretched out on the bench and closed my eyes. The sun felt so good, and I felt something ease in my chest as I rested.

9

A few minutes later, just as I was about to need to make a decision about a nap there in public, the dogs almost pulled my leg out of joint as they bolted toward something north on the water's edge. I sat up, whipped the leashes off my ankle before they dragged me like I was a prisoner in some old Western, and stood up to see what they were looking at.

At first, I didn't think much of it. Looked like a man was fishing down by the water, maybe even casting a net. I thought that might be illegal here, but I didn't know fishing regulations well and didn't really care enough about that infringement, if it even was one, to confront a random person on a deserted stretch of river front.

But the dogs wouldn't stop pulling, even when I hauled them back and put my hands on their heads. I studied the pups for a second and realized, surprisingly, that they weren't barking. Typically, they were the epitome of all bark and no bite, but today, they seemed ready to attack but didn't want to warn their victim.

I brought them to heel with some force on their leashes,

and then we walked up the paved path slowly toward the man. My plan, loosely formed at best, was to stroll by like we were just taking a walk, see if I could get a look at what was going on, and then leave it at that. I figured the man had probably just gutted some fish there, and the dogs were looking for a disgusting but tasty snack of fish innards.

As usual, the dogs seemed to sense my intention, and while they stayed on high alert, they also didn't pull or make even a loud snuffle as we approached the man.

He was bent over right at the water's edge, which is why my first impression had been that he was casting a net, not throwing a line. But as I got closer, I could see he was actually wrapping a rope around something, something soft and brown from the looks of it. That seemed odd, but people do odd things all the time.

It was only when I saw him tie big rocks from the river's edge onto the ends of the rope that I put it all together. He was trying to sink something. No one tried to bury something in water if they weren't up to something, ahem, fishy.

I tugged the dogs, hoping to move them along more quickly so we could get out of sight and call Jared, but Taco refused to budge. I pulled his leash, and he simply sank down to a crouch. And then he began to growl.

If anyone ever tries to tell you that Basset Hounds are easy-going dogs, be sure to call them out for fraud. They are lazy. They are cuddly. They are adorable. But they are also the most stubborn canines I have ever met, and I think Taco may have been the breed standard for that trait. He simply would not move.

The man didn't appear to have heard the growling yet, so I took a few steps back to the Basset and tried to lift him up to get him moving. Apparently, he had grown suction cups on his belly because I couldn't pry him from his crouch. His muscles were stiff, and he did not want to move.

I glanced up at the man, hoping he was still too focused on what he was doing to see us, but apparently, the noise of a middle-aged woman trying to lift a sixty-pound dog had broken his focus. He was looking right at us.

I stared a second as my brain caught up to my eyes. It was Roger Birmingham.

With a level of acumen I was surprised to have at the moment, I smiled and raised one hand to wave while I continued to try and lift Taco from the asphalt. "Good afternoon, Mr. Birmingham," I said with a strain caused my fear and physical exertion. "Taco here is apparently very eager to meet you."

It was only when he forced a smile that I realized Birmingham had been glowering at me. And the transition to stiff grin wasn't really less intimidating. In fact, I was now feeling scared for the first time. "Hi, Ms. Beckett. Out for a walk?"

"Indeed. Gorgeous day." I looked out over the water as my mind raced. "Catch anything?"

He glanced behind him to where I could just see the rock-laden end of the rope. "Not yet. Still some daylight left, so I'm hopeful." He started to walk up the brief incline toward me.

At this point, Taco stood and let forth a bark and a growl that further pushed my alarm system into high alert. When Mayhem came to stand against my leg and bared her teeth, my heart began to run even faster.

I held both of the dogs' leashes in my left hand, and fortunately, I had my right-hand in my pocket with my phone. By some great gift of cognitive firing, I remembered that if I held the button on the side of my phone down, the phone would automatically call 911. So I did that now. I felt the machine buzz in my fingers, and I let go, hoping someone had picked up on the other end.

I forced another smile. "Not sure what's up with them today. Sorry about this," I said as I shifted my weight and breathed a little sigh of relief when the dogs moved with me. "I'd better get them home. Good luck with your fishing."

Birmingham had stopped approaching when the dogs got aggressive. He was about five feet away, just distant enough that if the dogs lunged they couldn't reach him on their leash. "Thanks, Ms. Beckett. I hope you have a good day, too," he said. It was only then that I noticed the knife tucked into his leather belt.

I waved as casually as I could and turned the dogs to walk away. They obeyed, thank goodness, but they did keep sounding alert barks as we walked, their heads swiveling every few feet to be sure we weren't being followed.

For my part, I listened hard behind me and trusted the dogs to alert me if Birmingham followed. I figured I needed to look casual, even if my dogs didn't.

We made it to the end of the next street north, and I quickly steered the dogs back into the residential area. As we approached the end of the block, Taco suddenly stopped, turned around, and began to howl like he was Stephenie Meyer's latest werewolf creation. I looked back and saw Birmingham driving up the street in his truck. I could not have walked faster than he was moving, and every alarm system in my body when off.

The dogs and I began to run and turned the next corner to the left so that we could get closer back to town. Birmingham followed suit, inching closer as the dogs and I continued to run full-tilt.

We went another two blocks and then Mayhem tugged us into a hard right up the next street. It was only then that I realized we were at the end of Jared's block, and as I saw his house come into view, the three of us sprinted even more quickly into his backyard and slammed the gate behind us.

I heard Birmingham's truck stop on the street, and I knew we only had a minute before he was through the gate and in the backyard. The dogs would definitely get between me and him, but with that knife, they wouldn't last long in that fight.

I ran us around to the back deck of Jared's house and remembered that Jared kept a key in a lockbox by the grill. He'd told me the combination was his birthday, so I fumbled to punch in the numbers, fished out the key, and then shoved it into the lock just as I heard the gate open beside the house.

The dogs and I were into the house with the door locked behind us in seconds. The three of us bounded through the kitchen and the dining room into the living and then out the front door in a matter of seconds. I'd let go of their leashes, and the three of us were bolting up the street, trying to reach the store before Birmingham realized we were no longer in the house.

As we reached Main, two police cars screeched to a halt beside us, and Jared leapt out of the first cruiser and ran to me. "Harvey!" he shouted as he hugged me to him.

Tuck grabbed the dogs' leashes and brought them over. "What's going on?"

Behind me, I heard a truck start and looked back just in time to see Birmingham do an illegal U-turn and screech up the street in the other direction. I was breathless and couldn't say much. "Birmingham. Chased. Knife."

Tuck shoved the leashes into Jared's hand and jumped back into his cruisers. With lights flashing and siren on, he took off after Birmingham's truck.

"Do you need to go with him?" I said as my breathing slowed.

"Yes, but first, we're getting you inside with other people." He put his arm around my shoulders and steered all three of us the two blocks up the street into my bookstore. There, he signaled to Marcus and Rocky to come over, gave me a hug, and then ran back out the door faster than I'd ever seen him move.

As Rocky slid a mug of chamomile into my hands and

Marcus filled the dogs' bowl with water, Stephen and Elle came to sit with me. No one talked for a few minutes as I pulled myself together and then explained what had happened. "I'm okay. Just scared," I said finally.

"Of course you are, honey," Stephen said as he put his head against mine. "We're bringing everyone in early," he said as he gave me a tight squeeze and looked at Elle. "You got her?"

"I do," Elle said as Rocky squeezed my arm and went back to her counter.

Marcus was ringing up a customer, Walter was still at the CTTT table, and I could see Henri talking to someone in the history section. I took a deep breath. Everything was fine. Everything was fine.

Within minutes, my parents were there and insisting that I add something a little stronger to my tea, an offer I did not turn down even though the bourbon burned a bit. Cate and Lucas came soon after followed by Pickle, Bear, and Woody, who were all dressed up, or as dressed up as they got when not at work or in the courtroom. "We're here to help," Woody said as he tugged on his leather vest. "I'd like to volunteer to join Jared and hunt that bas—"

I interrupted him with a laugh. "They've got it, Woody, but thank you. Maybe you could help Marcus?" I had no idea what Marcus might need help with. Clearly, though, Woody needed a project.

Pickle and Bear followed after him, and as my women friends gathered around me, I felt my heartrate slow to normal. I loved all my friends, but something about the presence of strong women who knew me well was always the best balm for my soul. Dad, who had always found groups of women a little disconcerting, gave me a quick hug and then wandered over to Walter and Stephen's table.

Cate pulled her chair next to me. "So you're okay?"

I took a shuddering breath and then nodded. "I am." The

ACF BOOKENS

dogs were settled right against my feet, and I smiled as I looked at them. "Thanks to them."

As Henri joined us, I repeated my story and let the words of anger and support from my closest girlfriends sink deep into me. I hadn't always been willing to accept help, but now, especially today, I needed all the moral support they could give me.

Rocky refilled my mug and then said, "Anyone feel like making sugar cookies for tonight?"

I stared at her for a second. "Really?"

"Yep, I brought all the ingredients and was going to do it myself in the kitchen, but out here is just as good," she said as she turned to grab two large, stainless steel bowls off the counter behind her.

I grinned. I loved baking and didn't have nearly enough time to do it as much as I wanted to, so I was totally in. If my clothes got covered in flour, which would certainly happen, I had enough time still to run home and change, something I might want to do anyway since my sprint through the streets had me feeling a little less than fresh at the moment.

Right then, though, I wanted to bake, so we took over four of the tables in the café and began to mix ingredients. I wanted to make witchy cookies, to go along with the theme, but Rocky only had triangle cookie cutters. So Mom and Henri took on the challenge of adding little rolls of dough to the bottom of the triangles to make witch hats.

Soon, we had several trays of cookies to go, one at a time, into Rocky's brand new compact oven in the back, and within minutes, the store smelled heavenly. That was, of course, the whole reason Rocky had bought the oven. "If cookies can sell houses, I expect they can sell themselves and books, too," she'd told me.

She was so right. People came over to buy hot cookies and even asked if Rocky did baking classes. I could see the wheels turning in her mind as she pondered her answer, and when she said, "Not yet, but stay tuned," I knew we were about to add something really special to the store's offerings.

We all had a blast coloring the cookies black with icing and then adding feathers and leaves and even an animal or two as decoration, and when it came time to eat them, they tasted even better than they smelled. "Your mom's recipe?" I asked.

"Of course," Rocky said. "She's going to be thrilled you like them."

"I'm pretty sure I'd like your mom's recipe for cardboard," Henri said with a laugh before turning to me. "Okay, now that you're all relaxed, I'm taking you home to get a quick rest, a new outfit, and a long drink. Mart is bringing a new wine cocktail."

I sighed. "Okay. Is everyone coming?" I looked around at my friends.

Mom shook her head. "Nope. We're here for the duration. Elle and I are going to take care of setting up the final touches for the reading, and Cate is adding a flourish or two to the store in her own special way." Mom winked at Cate, and I smiled. This was going to be something I was sure.

"You go, Harvey," Rocky said. "We'll get it all ready and see you back here to eat in an hour."

I glanced down at my watch and saw it was already four o'clock. Where had the afternoon gone? I took a deep breath, smiled at all my friends, and followed Henri out to her car, where I found Dad and the dogs waiting. "Figured they'd need dinner," he said.

"Thanks, Daddy," I said as I took their leashes. "See you soon."

He smiled as he turned to go back inside. He looked fine, but I could see the worry on his face. I felt bad about worrying him, but given that it was Roger Birmingham that had been the troublemaker, I decided to let that guilt go.

Jared had been texting off and on for the past couple of hours to let me know they were still looking for Birmingham.

Now, I looked down to read his latest message. "Found his truck, but not him. Headed back to the water to find what he was hiding."

I'd filled both men in, by text, about what we'd seen Birmingham doing at the water, and I'd tried to pinpoint roughly where he'd been standing in relation to the bench we'd been sitting on. I hoped they could get some answers by looking there.

Jared's next text to me said, "I'll see you in fifty-two minutes. Can't wait."

I grinned and then slid my phone back under my leg.

"Good news?" Henri asked as she glanced at my face.

"The best kind," I said.

In a fresh, blue shirt dress, my knee-high boots, and more make-up than was my typical, I was eager to be back for Harrow's reading and to see what kind of "décor" my friends and mother had arranged for me. As Henri drove me back up the street, I gasped. The entire front of the store had a porch of lights hanging out over the sidewalk. It looked magnificent.

My friends had wrapped thin boards with lights and then cantilevered them out by d the strands of light to the sign Woody had made and had just now outfitted with small cup hooks. "This way you can put up the lights when you want them for special occasions without much trouble," he said as I stood with tears in my eyes at the front door.

"Wow," I said and reached out my arms to hug as many of these people that I loved as I could. When they stepped back, I felt my breath catch in my throat because there was Jared in dark blue jeans, a button-down shirt, and a cowboy hat. I had never fancied myself a woman who would like a man in a cowboy hat, but holy cow, did I ever.

He stepped forward and handed me a bouquet of wildflowers and said, "You look amazing," and then gave me a lingering kiss. "May I be your date tonight?"

"I'd be sad if you weren't," I whispered as I kissed him again and had to force myself to pull away. "Will you escort me inside?" I asked, feeling a bit like I was going to my high school prom. Prom had not been my finest moment in high school, so it was kind of nice to think of this moment as a new chance.

As soon as we stepped inside, though, all thoughts of high school gymnasiums fled my mind as I looked around at the way as strands of Edison bulbs hung in drapes over the stage. In front of the stage, was a newly constructed craftsman-style proscenium to frame the stage. It was decorated with hand-drawn flowers and leaves that fit the autumn season. It looked amazing and gave the reading space a bit more formality to set it off for a special night.

"It's collapsible, so we can slip it in the back room at the end of the night. And we've already got plans for the winter decorations and early spring, too," Cate said as she leaned against me. "Do you like it?"

"Like it?" I said as I squeezed Jared's hand and then let it go so I could hug her. "I love it." I stepped forward and studied the decorations. "You drew all of these?"

She blushed. "I've been working on it for a couple of weeks."

"Wow," I said. "Thank you." Over and over again, my friends stunned me with their kindness. I needed to find a way to repay them for all the ways they stood beside and behind me, but tonight, I was just going to be grateful.

Walter and Stephen stepped over and took me by the arm. "Now, it's time for you to eat." They steered me toward the back room, and when Stephen opened the door, I laughed out loud. They'd even decorated in here, but this time the theme was a bit more zany, with wry Jack-O-Lanterns, goofy scarecrows, and even a cackling witch in the corner.

Once I looked past the décor, though, I saw that the table was loaded with a veritable treasure trove of fall-themed food. I spotted pumpkin pie and stewed apples right away, and when I saw my mom's signature marinated pork loin, I felt my mouth begin to water.

Jared came up behind me and gently steered me toward the food. "I made these," he said as he picked up a dinner roll and slipped it onto his plate and winked at me.

"You made yeast rolls while you were chasing down someone who was threatening me today?" I eyed him curiously.

"Okay, I made the dough and had it ready to go, but I asked Cate to finish the proofing and baking for me," he said with a little blush. "I had more important things to do."

I nodded. "Well, I appreciate both your focus on my safety and your forethought to finish the rolls." I put one on my plate and followed it with a considerable pat of butter before loading up with the rest of the goodies, including some green beans that were so vibrant that I knew Elle had to have grown them.

As each person filled our plates, we found seats around the room and enjoyed a few moments of silent appreciation for the great food. I was dying to ask Jared about what had happened at the river today, but since he didn't bring it up and no one else did either, I decided to follow their lead and leave all talk about the afternoon until after the reading. I didn't want to spoil the festive mood, and I also didn't want to get myself all riled up again.

Instead, I asked which of Harrow's books my friends had read already, and soon, they were in the midst of an intense debate about which of her novels was the best. I had my own opinion, of course, and I'd tattooed my preference on my arm, but some of my friends were fans of her other books. I respected that, and I was especially thrilled that they were all going to meet her. And her them.

As soon as we were all done eating, I went out to the floor to give Elle and Marcus a break, and I was delighted to find Mart with Rocky in the café. "Dogs all squared?"

"Oh yes. I plied them with their usual kibble and a little of the roast beef in the fridge." She pointed toward their dog beds across the building by the stage. "I predict they will snooze through the entire reading. I hope Harrow doesn't mind the accompaniment of snoring."

I laughed as I saw my two hounds draped over their beds like they were the king and queen of the store, which of course they were.

Mart had picked my outfit tonight, laying it out at Henri and Cate's request before I even got home. Then, she'd done my hair with some magical method of using bobby pins to contain some curls and emphasize others. When Henri had then added her flare for make-up, I felt like I was at some low-key spa, and by the time they were done, I was more relaxed than I'd been all day. Given Jared's reaction combined with my own feelings about their attention, I figured I might be asking them to be my personal appearance team before every event at the store from now on.

While Marcus, Rocky, and Mart went back to get dinner, Elle and I staffed the café and bookstore. I got to try my hand a steamed milk heart, which didn't look much like a heart – more like a dinosaur – when I was done but still elicited oohs and aahs from the customer. I loved someone who was easily pleased.

As my friends finished up their meals and came back out onto the floor, it became clear to me that they had been marshalled, probably by my mother, into a clear plan of action. Pickle and Bear went outside and moved their cars from the spaces right in front of the store and replaced them with cones so that Harrow could park by the door. Lucas, Woody, and Dad patrolled the shop again picking up dirty cups and moving unshelved books to the library cart by the register. Meanwhile, Mart and Elle reshelved the books almost as quickly as the men brought them over, and Mom took first a spray bottle and clean cloth to the café tables and then a dust rag to the bookshelves.

Because Marcus, Rocky, and I were not given any specific chores, we did our usual, and I wandered the store speaking to customers and eventually made my way to where Walter and Stephen were packing up their Coming to the Table supplies. "How did it go?" I asked.

"Really well," Walter said. "We doubled our goal just from the regular folks who came by." Then he winked at Stephen.

"But your parents put us to quadruple our goal with their personal gift," he smiled at me with a huge grin, "in your honor."

I sighed. "They didn't?"

"Oh yes they did." Walter waved a check with my parents' names on it in front of my face. "We already talked to the director. This money is going to be used for a scholarship in your name for the next CTTT National Gathering in June."

I blushed. A scholarship in my honor. I didn't know quite what to say. "I'll thank them." Then I hugged my friends. "And thank you."

After I helped the guys pack up their table, I began to wander the store, and it was only then that I realized I hadn't seen Jared in a bit. I looked in the back room and then searched the aisles. I was just about to ask Woody to check the men's bathroom when he appeared from the back door. "I was worried," I said, and it was only when I heard the shrill pitch to my voice that I realized I was clearly still pretty worked up over the past few days' events.

"Oh, babe, I'm so sorry. I just stepped out to talk to Tuck. I should have told you," he pulled me into his arms.

I shook my head. "I don't know why I'm so worked up. You

really don't need to report on your whereabouts every minute." I meant what I said, but my heart was still racing.

"I know that," he said against the top of my head, "but I've made you worry a lot this week already, and then today, with Birmingham . . ."

"Yeah, but everything's okay, right?" I said into his chest.

"Everything's fine. I'll tell you all about everything after Harrow's reading. Tuck and Lu will be here in just a few minutes." He pushed me away so he could look into my face. "Are you okay?"

I cleared my throat and nodded. "I am. But is it weird if I ask you to stay close tonight? I kind of need to see your face, I think."

"Not weird at all. Flattering actually." He gave me a quick kiss. "Now, what else needs to be done?"

I looked around as we walked to the front of the store. "Not much. Everyone has been amazing." I glanced toward the café and saw Mom and Rocky setting out carafes of lemonade and our sugar cookies. "But it looks like we could help there." I pointed.

"Do I get to sample?" Jared said as we walked over.

"Of course," Mom said and handed him a cookie with a huge heart on it. "You're one of the family now, so you get the first cookies."

I blushed from my toes to my head because I knew my mom was almost as in love with Jared as I was and that her use of the word *family* and the heart cookie were not casual slips. Jared, however, didn't seem to notice what with his deep and undying affection to the cookie in his hand. So I took a deep breath. "More trays to carry out?" I tried to ask casually.

"Yep, six more," Rocky said and took me by the arm. "Your mom is something."

"Something is right," I said with a smile. "Thanks for this, by the way. What are we charging for these?"

"Pfft," Rocky said. "These are a gift for my new favorite author and one of my favorite people, too." She gave my shoulders a squeeze. "But coffee is for sale if you want to announce that.

"Absolutely," I said. "You have some help if things get busy?"

"Right here," Mart said as she joined us in the kitchen. "I'm your part-time barista for the night."

I smiled. "We're going to have to pay you if you work here more, you know?"

"Seriously," Rocky added.

"Are you kidding? The opportunity to simply ring up customers and make lattes is a delight after wrangling half-drunk wine tasters." Mart smiled. She loved her job, but she also had lots of good stories to tell about the infrequent wine snobs and far more frequent tipsy middle-aged moms who came into the tasting room.

I heard the bell tinkle over the door, and I turned to see Alix Harrow walking in. She looked elegant and comfortable in a pair of cream-colored, wide-legged trousers and a rust-colored blouse. Her hair was clipped back with simple black barrettes, and her make-up was bright but casual, too. In short, she looked like a woman out for a night with good friends, which was perfect.

"Oh, Ms. Harrow, it's so good to see you," I said.

"Harvey, if you don't start calling me Alix, we're going to have a problem," she replied with a smile.

"Does that mean you'll cast a spell on her?" Mart asked as she put out her hand. "I'm Mart."

"Nice to meet you, Mart, and alas, I do not have the abilities of my characters, I'm afraid. But if I did, I couldn't conjure up a nicer venue for this reading." She looked around at the lights and decorations. "Are those cookies for tonight?"

Rocky grinned. "They are. Made special for you and your books."

Alix took a step closer and smiled. "They're perfect. May I?"

"Of course," Rocky said and held up a platter.

Alix took her time choosing her cookie and finally settled on a witch's hat decorated with tiny blue and yellow flowers. Then, she set the cookie down, propped a copy of *Once and Future Witches* against the tray next to it and snapped a photo. "I'll get this up right now."

I walked with our guest over to the stage and watched as she snapped more pictures and immediately loaded them to Instagram. "This is amazing, Harvey," she said as she slipped her phone back into her purse. "Wow."

"My friends did all of it." I pointed to where they were huddled like schoolgirls at their first dance. "They're also big fans."

Alix smiled. "Do they have books they'd like me to sign before I get prepped for the reading?"

"Are you kidding?" I said. "Watch this."

I walked over to the giggling coterie of men and women and said, "Alix," I put a lot of emphasis on her name with a smile, "has offered to sign your books before the reading as a thanks for all your work. You know, if any of you are interested."

Henri and Pickle both literally jumped into the air, and Cate clasped a hand over her mouth like I'd just told her Santa Claus was coming. Then, they all scattered to where they'd left their belongings around the stage and quickly lined up in front of Alix.

"I feel like I'm the water fountain after recess," Alix said with a laugh as she reached out and took Elle's book. "To whom should I make it out?"

Elle flushed and said, "Elle, please – E L L E."

As my friends queued up to fawn over their fav, I walked over to where Jared, Lu, and Tuck were talking in the corner. "She has some die-hard fans now, thanks to you, Harvey," Tuck said.

"I have created monsters," I said with a laugh. "She's incredibly generous. But if we can, let's keep her oblivious to all the goings on."

"Definitely," Jared said. "Not a word about anything at all tonight." He winked at me, and I felt my stomach do a little flip.

"I better go get my book signed, too," Lu said as she pulled *The Thousand Doors of January* out of her purse.

I laughed. "Another one," I said.

"Seriously, I even read them, and you know I don't read new books," Tuck said. "They were amazing."

"Maybe you should get in line, too, Sheriff?" Jared said with a chuckle.

THE CROWD BEGAN FILLING in the seats before six-fifteen. Fortunately, Marcus had moved a comfortable chair, a small table, and a footstool into the back room, so Alix had a decaf latte, a second cookie, and some peace and quiet while the room filled. I peeked in from time to time to check on her, but she was contentedly reading her own choice of book, *A Psalm for the Wild-Built*, while she waited.

Promptly at seven, I walked her to the stage, stood at the microphone and welcome seventy-eight people to the reading. The reading area was packed to the fire code limit. The crowd was enthusiastic but respectful, and when Alix decided to read from her newest title, a teenage girl in the back row cheered with delight.

Alix's reading was perfect. She took questions with wit and grace, and when the line to sign snaked around the room, she only smiled and picked up her pen. After an hour, the line was gone, and she was ready to head back to her hotel. "Thank you so much, Harvey. I had a blast, and now I need to sleep."

"Of course, Alix. Thank you so much for coming." I gave her a hug, invited her back anytime, and then watched as my dad walked her to her car out front. Then, I turned to my friends gathered behind me and pumped the air with my fist. "Yes!" I shouted. "Now, do you mind helping me clean up?"

Clean up wasn't complicated, except by the fact that we were all tired. But since even all the cookies and lemonade were gone, and so were most of Harrow's books, I expected everyone had enjoyed themselves. From the look on Rocky's tired but smiling face, she had done well in the café for the evening, too.

As my friends put in even more effort to tuck away the chairs and clean up the remnants of the evening, I ran the totals on the register to find that we had beaten all sales records that day. I stacked the few copies of each of Harrow's titles left in the store so that they could be scooped up tomorrow. She'd graciously signed them before she left, so I knew they wouldn't be here past tomorrow.

It had been a long day with a stellar ending, and when everyone left with hugs and kisses for each other, all I wanted was to have Jared walk me home and sit with me on the couch. When he leashed up the dogs and said, "Ready?" I had to resist the urge to shout my yes.

10

T he night air was cool and breezy, and somehow that felt perfect, like it was lifting something inside me that needed to be buoyed a bit before I heard the stories from the harder part of the day. I linked my arm with Jared's as we walked, and finally, I said, "Okay, tell me."

He tucked my arm in tighter and took a deep breath. "Birmingham was able to elude Tuck long enough to ditch his truck, as you know. We expect he called someone to come pick him up."

I sighed. Nothing comforting about the man being aided by someone. Still, I hoped the next part of Jared's information would be good news. "And at the river?" I prompted.

"Well, it's not exactly good news, but it is good information. We found Catherine Birmingham's purse right where you said it would be. He hadn't even thrown it very far into the water." Jared's voice was quiet, like he was thinking about something.

"He was too busy trying to chase me down, I guess," I said.

Jared glanced over at me. "Yeah, probably." He sounded far less certain than I felt. "At the very least, it ties him to her murder."

I nodded as we walked up to my door and went inside to find Mart and Symeon on the couch with glasses of wine. "Pour me one of those while I change?" I asked no one in particular.

"On it," Mart said.

"Maybe you can catch them up?" I said to Jared as I turned down the hallway toward my room.

I heard him explain what they'd found about Birmingham's truck and Catherine's purse as I slid into fleece pajama bottoms and a comfy T-shirt. When I came back out, Mart had set my glass of white wine on the coffee table, and I picked it up as I slid in next to Jared on the end of the couch. "What did I miss?"

"Nothing, actually, because I wanted to get your opinion on something," Jared said. When I nodded, he continued. "Clearly Birmingham was hiding something."

All three of us nodded.

"But not well." Jared looked at me. "I mean if you really wanted to lose a purse in water, there are much bigger, deeper, more isolated stretches of river and bay around here. Why pick a place right by a trail in the middle of town?"

"Expediency?" Symeon suggested.

"Laziness?" Mart added with a roll of her eyes.

"You wouldn't," I said. "You think he wanted someone to find the purse?"

Jared shrugged. "I don't know, but it seems odd that if he was trying to hide it there and then, even if he wanted to catch you, he didn't take the additional three seconds he would have needed to toss the purse into the middle of the river."

I sat back and sipped my wine as I pondered Jared's train of thought. He had a point, and if I hadn't been so terrified, I might have thought of it myself. But I was still stuck on something, "Why chase us though?"

"I have a theory about that, too," Jared said as he winked at me.

"My stunning good looks," I said with more levity than I felt.

"Well, who could blame him?" Jared said as he leaned over and kiss my cheek. "But I suspect it had more to do with wanting to either scare you for the sake of appearances or so that you would do exactly what you did and call the police."

Mart leaned forward from where she and Symeon sat on the chair and a half by the fire. "Are you saying that he terrorized Harvey for the sake of appearances?"

Jared shook his head. "It's awful either way, and I have no proof. But something isn't adding up here."

I had to admit I thought Jared was right, now that I wasn't running for my life. "But he broke into your house. That's pretty serious commitment to a farce."

"That's the thing; he didn't break in. No windows were broken, and the door was still locked when I checked this afternoon." He looked at me pointedly. "I think he went right back out the gate once you were inside."

I stared at my boyfriend. "He didn't follow me in?"

Jared shook his head.

"Wow. Well, then he certainly could have caught me if he was just waiting in the side yard when I came out the front." I let out a long, slow breath. It looked like Jared was onto something, but I didn't feel any better at all knowing that fact.

I SLEPT FITFULLY THAT NIGHT, so when my alarm went off at seven, I pulled myself out of bed and headed straight for coffee. The guys had left about eleven, and while we had offered to let them stay, one on the couch and one in the guest room, they'd both declined with the assertion that we'd all sleep better if we were in our own beds.

Now, I was glad to have the house to myself. Jared's theory seemed even more likely in the fresh light of morning, but it meant that the idea that Birmingham had killed his daughter was probably completely off-base. What *that* meant, however, I couldn't figure.

As I put bread into the toaster and celebrated a small win that our butter bell was actually full of fresh, soft butter, Kara Birmingham's very public confrontation on the street yesterday came to mind. I had thought she was just livid because she was in the throes of grief and maybe guilt about her daughter's death, but now I was wondering if she had been putting on a show, too.

I picked up my phone to text Jared about that idea but decided that if, by chance, he was taking a rare morning to sleep in – as he so much deserved – I didn't want to wake him, especially not with some half-formed theory that might not even pan out. It could wait.

With my buttered toast, my coffee, and my new read, *The Mermaid's Child*, I settled into my reading chair to enjoy an hour of mental quiet before I really launched into my day. The experience was, as it always was on the days when I let myself go fully into a book, blissful, and by the time I forced myself to stop reading and get ready for work, I felt more rested and steady than I had all week. I was sure, from my reading about anxiety and brain science, that there was something about eye movement and distraction involved in the way I felt rested after reading, but today, I was going to chalk it up to magic, the mermaid kind.

At nine as I headed out the door, I heard a wolf whistle and looked out at the road to find Jared waiting for me. He was back in flannel, and the shadow of beard on his face made him even more gorgeous than usual. "What are you doing here?" I said as I walked over.

"Until we know what's going on for sure, I'm walking you to and from work, Sheriff's orders and my pleasure." He reached over and took the dogs' leashes from me, shifted them to his right hand, and then took mine with his left. "Did you sleep?"

I nodded. "Not particularly well, but I did sleep. You?"

"Same. But this morning, I spent some time with Nicholson Baker, and I feel much better." Jared was reading through all of Baker's work, and he loved it, as odd and deep as it could be.

I smiled. "I read Jo Baker and had the same experience." I felt a deep warmth in my chest that this man I loved found his way in books as much as I did.

We walked on for a couple of blocks, and then I said, "I did have a theory about Kara Birmingham, though."

"You think she made that scene on purpose?" he asked with a small smile.

"You thought of that, too." I nodded. "Of course you did."

"Tuck called Kara this morning to ask her to come into the station to answer some questions about her husband. He told her it's about his incident with you yesterday, and he will ask about that," Jared spoke quietly as he scanned to be sure no one was in ear shot.

"But he also wants to ask if they are in danger?"

Jared grinned. "You are good at this." He gave me a kiss on the cheek.

"Too many novels," I said. "Any word on where Birmingham is at this point?"

"Nothing. But there are other things in the works to see if we can get more information." Jared winked at me.

"Things I need to be kept in the dark about?" I said.

"For your own good," he whispered against my ear. "But it's all under control."

I took a deep breath, forced myself to be grateful for my ignorance, and changed the subject before I thought too much about what "under control" might mean in this scenario. "So what's your plan for the day?"

He pulled a copy of *The Mezzanine* out of his back pocket

and said, "Reading while I watch the most amazing woman in the world work."

I laughed. "You're going to stay at my store all day?"

"Is that okay?" he said as he raised his eyebrows and watched me unlock the door.

"Totally okay by me as long as you sit where I can gaze at you while I work." I stretched up and kiss him before going to turn off the alarm.

When I came back to the front of the store, he had moved one of the arm chairs right onto the center of the stage and was leaning back, boots propped on a small stool, with his book in his lap. "Will this do?"

I laughed. "Perfect," I said and then laughed out loud when he picked up his book and started to read right there on display for me and the world. I loved it.

BY NOON when Marcus joined me in the shop, I had already sold out of Harrow's remaining copies, moved a fair number of books from the "Similar to Harrow" display that Marcus had set up quickly last night, and also placed a number of orders for her books. She was now a hit with the St. Mariner's, and I could not blame them one bit.

Because Jared had remained in the center of the stage, only leaving for coffee and bathroom breaks, Marcus had set up a sign next to him that said, "Ask Jared about his favorite books," and several customers had done just that. I was going to ask him later what he'd recommended, but the one suggestion I did hear went to a little boy in boots much like my boyfriend's who wanted something adventurous to read.

"Have you read *Tristan Strong Destroys The World?*" Jared asked.

The little boy shook his hair and his dreadlocks tapped against his cheeks. "Does he really destroy things?"

"He really does, but he's a hero. Want me to show you where it is?" Jared looked up at the boy's father, who nodded. "This way."

I watched the three of them head to the middle grade section and let myself flush with delight. This man was amazing – not perfect – but amazing, and I could not believe I got to be with him. Just the thought made my heart flip over.

But despite the good sales day and Jared's continually handsome presence on the stage, I couldn't keep my mind from sliding over to the Birminghams and Dooley and what all this might mean. I was so eager to know what was going on with Tuck and the "under control" activity that Jared had hinted at, but I trusted that Jared would tell me anything crucial and that anything he didn't tell me really was for my own good.

Fortunately, the store was very busy, so I asked Jared to grab us all lunch so we could eat in shifts and keep the floor fully staffed. When he came back with burgers and fries from the food truck that parked outside the big Methodist church in Easton, I grinned. They were delicious and the perfect food for a day when I was tired but invigorated.

Sales were steady throughout the day, and I was glad to see that Rocky's assistant had come in for the afternoon so she could get a break. Rocky had been here all day every day this week, and I didn't want her to burn out.

About three, when things started to slow down, I sent Marcus home, too. He'd worked more hours than I had this week, and while he was always good natured and energetic, his steps were a little slower than usual. We were closing up at five today, so I assured him I could handle the next two hours. He smiled and was on the phone to Rocky before he even got out the door. I hoped they'd enjoy a few hours together away from our store.

When Marcus left, Jared sauntered over and said, "Did I hear you're closing at five?"

"We are. I just hung the sign in the window. It's usually slow for those last couple of hours anyway, and I'm beat." I took a minute to lean back against the counter behind me and let myself feel the fatigue.

"I'm delighted you're taking care of yourself, and since I'm well into my second book now," he held up a copy of *The Little Prince*, "I feel very good saying that I'd like to relax with you on my couch while we watch something appropriately Halloween-like."

"Like scary? Or gory?" I asked with a little wariness.

"Scary only. Have you seen *Get Out?*"

I shook my head, "I hear it's amazing and terrifying though."

"Oh, it is, but I'll hold you close, okay?"

I blushed and nodded. Nothing sounded better.

As Jared finished his second book of the day up on the stage, I prepped for the week ahead by printing our pull sheets of books to return, putting in our order for the week, and thinking about window displays that we could swap in now that Harrow's event was over.

Tuck was doing his meet and greet on Tuesday, so I decided something about police procedurals would be fitting and not too "on the nose." As I pulled titles from the shelves so that Marcus could make the display the next day, my mind wandered to what exactly Jared had been alluding to earlier.

I tried to convince myself that he was just talking about Tuck's intended conversation with Kara Birmingham, but I knew that wasn't it. He had already told me that was happening, so something else was going on.

I texted Mart. "Symeon with you?"

"Yep, at a winery. You okay?"

"Totally fine. Just working on a theory."

"Oh Lord," Mart replied with an eyeroll emoji. "Be careful."

"Jared's here."

"Of course he is," she said.

So it wasn't that Symeon had gone back undercover. I kept thinking as I began to carry the stack of books to the front window to make it easier for Marcus. Then, I tripped and the stack and I went tumbling across the floor.

Jared was by my side in a flash, and after he helped me to my feet, saw that nothing but my pride was bruised, and gathered the books back into the stack, he said, "It's four forty-five. Let me help you finish up?"

I knew he'd been resisting the urge to help me all day – that was just his nature – but I so appreciated that he gave me space to do my job and that he took the time to enjoy something he loved, even as he sort of did his job, too.

"Sounds good. Can you put those inside the front window for me?"

He nodded and headed that way as I did a final sweep of the store to let the few remaining customers know that we were closing in a few minutes and to pick up the books scattered on tables around the shop. Normally, I would try to shelve those before I went home, but since I was opening in the morning and Mondays were typically a little slower, I decided to give myself a break and let them live on the library cart overnight.

As Jared helped Cecilia do a final wipe down of the tables and then invert the chairs so she could mop, I rang up the final customers and then flipped off the open sign and locked the door.

Within minutes, the café floor was clean, the register closed out, and the store shut down for the night. It was getting dark, and so I was glad the walk to Jared's was short. Well, at least it was short distance-wise. The snuffling and peeing of two pups meant that it took us a little longer than usual to get there, what with the weaving back and forth to check out various scents.

As soon as we walked in, I smelled them – churros. Lu was here. My friend always smelled like cinnamon and honey, but when you added in the scent of fried dough, I knew she was cooking. "Tuck and Lu are here?" I asked.

"Just for a bit, to eat and give us the run-down on the day. If you mind, I can ask them to go," he said with a touch of worry on his brow.

I smiled and kissed him. "It's great. I've been dying to know what was going on, and while I do look forward to that movie later, I'll probably be able to concentrate on being scared and comforted more fully if I'm not distracted." I gave him a wink.

He grinned and said, "Oh good. I knew you'd be wondering, so I thought it might be okay."

"Totally okay," I said as I took his hand and pulled him into the kitchen. "Especially if Lu made churros."

Lu laughed. "Of course, I did. After a week like this, we all need a little sweet fried goodness." She then gestured to the rest of the meal. "But Tuck made us all a salad bar to balance it out."

I looked over at Tuck and said, "You can cook?"

"Do you see anything cooked here?" he asked as he handed me a plate.

"Point taken," I said and made myself a salad with lots of mixed greens, cucumbers, olives, shredded cheese, chickpeas, and sesame seeds. When I added a dollop of Catalina dressing, I smiled. This was exactly the salad I made every day for lunch in college, and I had missed it.

We sat down in Jared's dining room, and Tuck asked me how the day had gone. I told him it had been a normal day except for the hot guy who refused to get off my stage, and we all had a good laugh at Jared's antics.

Then, Lu said, "Alright, enough small talk. How is Woody?"

I looked from her to Tuck and then said, "Woody? What about Woody?"

Jared squeezed my knee under the table and kept his hand there. I tried to focus on the warmth to stay calm.

"Woody went undercover for us today with Dooley," Tuck said just before he filled his mouth with a large forkful of salad.

I glared at him, knowing he wouldn't speak with his mouth full and had intentionally made me wait to ask my slew of follow-up questions.

Fortunately, Jared spared me the delay and said, "One of Dooley's men approached him last night before the reading. Woody was shelving books in the Civil War section, and the man apparently thought he might be a like-minded individual, started talking to him about States' Rights as the sole cause of the Civil War, and then went into the hate group nonsense."

I growled low in my throat and didn't even realize I was doing it until Mayhem's collar jangled beside me. She was looking at me to see what was wrong. "Sorry, girl," I said and patted her head. "Go on," I said to Tuck.

"Fortunately, Woody thought fast and played along. Said he was so tired of all this political correctness or something that sent the right signals, and when the guy asked why he was at this particular bookstore, Woody said, and I quote, 'Got to keep your enemies closer, right?'"

I raised my eyebrows. "Wow, he did think fast on his feet. So they recruited him?"

Jared nodded. "Told him to be at the clubhouse at eight a.m. So we got him wired up and Tuck spent the day listening in."

"And?" I said impatiently.

Lu chuckled.

"He got in to the inner circle," Tuck said with an ominous voice.

"You make it sound like it's some sort of secret society of werewolves," Lu said.

"It kind of is," Jared said without a smidgen of humor.

I cringed. "What does that mean?"

"One of Dooley's men told him that they thought Birmingham wasn't trustworthy," Tuck said. "Said they were keeping an eye on him because they thought he might crack."

I looked at Jared. "You were right."

Jared nodded. "I was, and now I feel like we're in some movie where there's a whistleblower who we have to protect but can't because they're on the run."

"That would make a great movie," Lu said. "But what do you do next?"

I groaned, and Mayhem sat up again. "Woody's going back in isn't he?"

Jared nodded. "He is. And taking Pickle. Apparently, he hinted to the guys that Pickle might also be inclined to help Dooley's campaign."

"And they believed him?" Lu asked. "Pickle is the most liberal lawyer around."

"Woody is a stellar liar. He told them that he works for people who need help with the snowflake system, so he has to seem like a snowflake to be good at his job." Tuck grinned as he relayed this bit of detail.

I rolled my eyes. "And these men are so gullible that they believed that?"

"Not hard to convince people are conspiring when they feel like they're being conspired against," Jared said. "So tomorrow they're all going out to where Birmingham is hiding out to see what they can find out, and they invited Woody along."

"So they are hiding Birmingham?" I asked.

Jared nodded. "Woody thinks it may be more of a captive situation, though, so we'll be close."

I sighed. "Birmingham called Dooley's men for help, thinking it would help build him cover, but instead, they were already suspicious of him." In the course of a few minutes, my feelings about this man had changed markedly. "He's in danger."

Tuck sighed. "It appears so, and we need to know what he knows and how he got so far into Dooley's circle."

"Which means we need to get him out," Jared said.

I put my head down on my arms and took a deep breath. First Symeon, then Jared, and now Woody and Pickle . . . the danger the people I loved were in was getting to me. After a few moments, I lifted my head and said, "Okay, so how are you keeping Woody safe?"

The men went through the procedures they had in place, including the wire, their presence nearby at all time, and the addition of two part-time deputies to help out in town while Jared and Tuck focused solely on Woody and his time with Dooley's crew.

I felt a bit better knowing what the plan was, but I was still profoundly nervous for Woody, and for Tuck and Jared, if I was honest. If Dooley and his men were capable of holding a man hostage, it seemed they were probably willing to do most anything to get what they wanted.

"What does Dooley want, though? What could Birmingham possibly know that would be such a threat?" I asked.

Jared and Tuck exchanged a look, and my heart quickened. I looked over at Lu who shook her head. Tuck hadn't clued her in on something crucial either.

After a moment of silence, Tuck nodded, and Jared said, "Inside Catherine's purse, we found her phone, and she had made a lot of calls to Dooley and he to her."

The silence in the room got very heavy for a few moments. "She and Dooley were in a relationship," I said quietly.

"Yes, for a few months now," Tuck said. "She had saved a few voicemails, and it seemed pretty serious."

I looked at him and then at Jared. "There's something else." I could feel the weight of what they weren't saying in the air.

Jared sighed. "Yes. She had saved some voicemails from him, some very angry voicemails."

"He killed her," Lu said.

Tuck nodded. "We think so. Apparently, she was not meeting Dooley's expectations for a girlfriend of the future sheriff."

"She was using?" I asked.

"Sounds like it," Jared continued. He then explained that Dooley had wanted Catherine to show up for events playing the proper role as his girlfriend and when she didn't show or came late, he lost it on her.

Lu sighed and then smiled softly at her husband. "Thank goodness you don't have those expectations of me."

He laughed. "Love, I know better than to demand your time and attention. I just consider it a gift that you give it to me."

She kissed him quickly and then stood up. "Churros?"

"Everything is easier with fried food and sugar, right?" I added and stood to help her. When the guys started to stand, too, I added, "Let us, just this once, serve you like you serve our community."

"I could get used to this," Jared said with a wink at me.

"Don't," I snapped back with my own wink.

While we ate dessert, we tried to keep things light even as we ran over the details for Tuck's meet and greet on Tuesday. I wanted it to be a fun evening, but I also wanted people to have a chance to really talk to Tuck if they needed his ear.

We decided to have some music playing and set out board games and puzzles for people to play. I would ask Rocky if she could make cookies again, and I'd buy them from her this time, and Lu planned on bringing over her homemade chips and salsa.

Jared offered to donate a side table he'd made as a door prize, and I said I'd pull together a gift bag of police procedurals as another prize, too. I figured Elle might give some flowers, and maybe Cate or Henri could give a piece of art. We'd make it night out for folks but also set up a private space for people to bend Tuck's ear for a few minutes if they wished.

"Can someone be the timekeeper though?" Lu asked. "I could see a chatty person taking up the whole evening with my too-kind husband."

Jared looked at me and winked. "Your mom would be great at that," he said.

I grinned. "You're totally right, and she'll relish the power."

By the time the Masons packed up their dinner supplies and headed out, we had a solid plan for Tuesday and had, largely it seemed, managed to not think about tomorrow's events at all. When Jared turned on the movie and then wrapped me up tight against his chest on the couch, all thoughts of anything but where I was right then left my mind completely.

11

W hen I got to the shop the next morning, I went right to work shelving the books from the night before and then beginning to pull the returns from this week's list. Normally, I hated this chore, but something about it today was enjoyable – maybe it was the focused attention it required, maybe the chance to really study the shelves and make notes about what we might add to our inventory, maybe just the distraction from what I knew was happening just outside of town.

Jared had texted me as I walked into work and let me know they were sitting near a cabin just south of town, where Woody had told them Birmingham was being held. Woody was inside with Dooley and two other men, and apparently, they were asking Birmingham why his wife had made such a big scene in town.

"Birmingham held the 'you know women' line well, and they seemed to buy it. But now they're talking about why he needed help on Saturday. Seems he called Dooley directly, and maybe that's a big no-no."

"Eek," I said. "Alright, you focus. Just check in and let me know everyone's okay?"

"Absolutely," he said and sent a kissing emoji.

It was ridiculous how much joy I got from that simple yellow face, but it made me warm all over, especially when I thought about the goodnight kiss Jared had given me at my door after he walked me home the night before.

After I opened the store, I was glad the stream of customers was steady but not too extreme. I needed some mental down-time even as I also needed the focus required for me to attend to people who needed my help. One woman about my age really wanted a novel that would let her disappear into a story and that she loved YA, and I was thrilled to be able to hand her the beautiful new box set of the His Dark Materials trilogy.

"Be forewarned though," I said. "I cried harder in book three than I ever have when reading."

She smiled. "Well, then, these sound perfect."

ABOUT ELEVEN-THIRTY, Jared texted me to say that everything was still fine. They'd followed Woody and some of the men as they'd been campaigning for the day, and nothing unusual had happened.

I sighed and tried to take respite in my friends' safety, but I also knew they were all really hoping that Woody would get the scoop on something, be it the Birminghams or the threats to Tuck. No news was only good news in so far as it went.

But by five p.m., my nerves were so frazzled that even the best pep talk about "no news" wasn't working, and when Marcus took over the store and the dogs and I walked home, I decided, in a very uncharacteristic move, to go for a jog.

The three of us went in, and while I changed into the quasi-workout clothes I had – sweat pants and a T-shirt – the dogs got a long drink and a short nap. Then, I leashed them up and took to the road in the hopes that wearing myself out might just help me wind down a bit.

I am not one of those people built for running. My legs don't move smoothly in any sort of form, and no matter how far I go, I don't usually hit any kind of zone that lets me forget I can't breathe. But because of those things, jogging is an all-encompassing act of mind and body, which is just what I needed.

By the time the dogs and I had run to the edge of town and back, I could feel my nervous system starting to calm, and my brain was no longer racing. As I came in the house, I made the decision to do exactly what I needed to do tonight, which involved an easy meal, a quick clean-up of the house, and then a couple of hours of TV before an early bedtime.

I put together a little plate of salami, cheese, olives, and apple slices, and as I put away the miscellaneous things that had accumulated on the counters and side tables over the past few days, I snacked and sipped a cranberry spritzer that I mixed up from some seltzer and the last of our cranberry juice.

Then, house tidy and body relaxed, I settled onto the couch with a blanket, a pillow, and *Roswell*. Alien life seemed just the thing to keep my attention while also not feeling too close to home.

When I woke up about nine-thirty to Mart calling my name softly, I sighed, hugged my friend, checked my phone to see that all was still well with Jared and friends, sent him a good night text, and went immediately to bed. It was blissful, and I don't think I moved all night.

The next morning when I woke up after a solid twelve hours of sleep, I felt great, and while that didn't mean I was inclined to go for another jog, I reminded myself that I needed some good physical activity to keep myself healthy and decided to talk to Mart about getting a spinning bike for us both.

But plans for fitness equipment would have to wait because

we had Tuck's event tonight, and I wanted everything at the shop to be perfect for him and to show those jerks who were out for him that he had friends and lots of support.

When I got to the store, Rocky was already there, and the building smelled amazing. I loved that when I was the first one in, I could still catch a tiny whiff of oil and gasoline from the days when the building was a gas station, but I didn't think most customers would appreciate that fragrance while they shopped for books. So the scent of freshly ground coffee beans and whatever deliciousness Rocky had in the oven were welcome.

I dropped off the dogs and my bag and headed over to say good morning. "You're here early," I said, trying to act as if that was unusual.

"I am, but that's because I won't be here all day. I'm taking most of the day off, so I just wanted to come in and make sure everything was set." She grinned at me.

With a smile, I leaned over the counter to give her a high five, "Love that. Big plans?"

"No, and that's the best part. I'm going to just go where the wind takes me." She grinned. "But I'll be back for Tuck's event. I wouldn't miss that for anything."

I nodded. "You still good to serve coffee?"

We talked for a few minutes about the more limited menu she'd have available for sale, and then I headed back into the shop to finish my chores.

Promptly at ten, I turned on the sign, unlocked the door, and opened it to find Jared smiling at me with a single yellow sunflower in his hand. "Good morning," he said as he leaned over to kiss me.

I closed my eyes and let the warmth of his kiss settle in before holding the door and saying, "Please, sir, come in. Can I help you find anything?"

He looked at me and winked, "I have found just what I'm

looking for." He leaned over and kissed me again. "You get a good night's rest?"

I told him about falling asleep on the couch and then going right to bed. "I even went for a jog," I said.

He winked. "So we can run together now?"

"Um, no," I said. "No we can't. Not unless you like running more slowly than you can walk and also going an eighth as far as usual."

He laughed. "Fair enough. Maybe we'll just stick to walks together." He kissed my cheek. "Have time for, um, more coffee?" He looked at the mug in my hands.

"If you're good with hanging by the register, sure thing." There weren't many customers yet on this chilly fall morning, and I really wanted to hear what had happened yesterday. "We can speak in code," I stage whispered.

He grinned. "Be right back."

A moment later, he was back with two mugs and a request from Rocky that I not become a mug hoarder for the sake of her bottom line. I shot her an eye roll as I took the final sip from my first mug and then immediately picked up the second. She laughed out loud.

After I rang up a man who was purchasing Ken Follett's entire The Pillars of the Earth series, I leaned my left hip against the counter and looked at my boyfriend. "Spill," I said.

He smiled. "I'm surprised you could sleep last night without the details."

"Hence the jog. I was so keyed up I had to find some way to manage." I stared at him over my second mug as I waited.

He stared back but finally said, "Our agent is fine and doing his usual today. But he did get some good information, and we're preparing to act on it."

I nodded and waited because I knew he wasn't going to give me only the police speak version. I kept waiting until I realized he was, indeed, only going to tell me that much. "That's it."

He scanned the store behind me and then pulled me to him. "There's a lot more," he whispered, "but for your own safety, I can't tell you." He kissed the top of my head and then stood back. "Sorry all of this interrupts our usual Tuesday lunch date."

I held his eyes for a minute, but when he didn't even blink, I knew I was at the end of the line in terms of information. "Okay, then." I was disappointed and a little hurt, even though I knew I wasn't being reasonable.

Jared frowned, but he didn't say anything further. He sipped his own coffee and waited.

I took a deep breath and a long pull of my latte, and then I thought about how it must make him feel to not be able to tell me everything. I knew that was hard, and though I was still disappointed, I decided to just let that go.

"You coming tonight?" I asked as I stepped forward and wrapped my arms around his waist.

He smiled at me gently. "Wouldn't miss it?" he said. "We'll all be here to support Tuck."

I stepped back. "All?"

"Some of the deputies from Easton said they were coming over," he said as he looked over my shoulder. "You have a customer."

I turned around in time to see a woman and a tiny infant walking over. She had a collection of Sandra Boynton board books in her hands, and I lost myself completely in a conversation about my favorite rhymes.

When I finished her sale, Jared came back from where he had returned his mug and my first one and said, "I'll see you tonight. Be here at five with dinner." He kissed my cheek, and I resisted the urge to hold him tight for a very long time.

"See you then," I said and watched him walk out the door and head toward the station. His movements were loose and fluid, but the pinched expression around his eyes told me there was something on his mind, something he couldn't tell me. I took a deep breath and forced myself to a calm place where my trust in him lived. Then, I went back to work.

AT FOUR-THIRTY, my parents, Cate, and Lucas came in with plates and such for dinner. Mom had let me know she had this part of our day under control, and while I felt bad again for relying on them for the second time in just a few days, I knew Mom loved it.

She set up the table in the break room like a buffet, and when the Chinese food from the shop up the street arrived, she laid it all out like a spread for royalty and steered first Marcus and then me into the back to eat. When Jared arrived just before five, he joined me to fill his plate, and we sat and talked about the afternoon he'd spent with the local Eagle Scout troop as they organized the file room at the station.

"I had no idea teenage boys could be so chatty," I said after he told me about how he'd learned everything about seemingly everyone at the high school in those three hours.

"Give them the right space, and they'll talk your ear off," Jared said with a laugh. "My mom used to joke that I wouldn't say much of anything until we were in the car, and then she just sat and listened to me jabber for the whole ride to where ever we were going."

"I bet she made up road trips just to hear you talk," I suggested.

"I suspect so. We did a lot of ice cream runs in those days," he said. After he wiped his mouth with his napkin, he said, "Now, what can I help with?"

"Well, Marcus is redoing the front window to make it all about Tuck, so he might need help there. And I definitely need help with chairs." I stood up and cleared our plates into the trashcan. "pick your poison."

"Well, if one of my options includes being with you, then you know what I'm choosing," he grinned and then turned his face serious. "Too much?"

I laughed. "Not at all, you romantic fool you." I kissed him slowly and then forced myself away and out the back room door. "You coming?"

"Just give me a minute to come back to earth," he said slowly as he ran a hand over his face. "I'll be right there."

I laughed as I pushed the cart of chairs into the store. We were going to set up a few small groupings of seats around the bookstore itself and let people gather there or in the café to talk. Cate and Elle were going to staff the table with the sign-up sheet where people could get a bit of Tuck's time, and Walter and Stephen were going to help them by having information about Tuck's campaign available.

As I began to create a small circle of chairs near the register, I saw Cate and Lucas had already flung a blue tablecloth over the folding table and were putting out a clipboard. "Looks great," I said.

"Thanks," said Lucas. "Fifteen minute slots?"

"I think that's plenty of time," I said.

"Me, too," Cate added and began to pencil in times on the sign-up sheet.

Over the course of the next few minutes, Walter and Stephen arrived with a large box full of campaign materials that they laid out first on Cate and Lucas's table and then spread to the smaller tables in the shop and café.

Stephen gave my arm a squeeze as he walked by, and I found myself a little emotional to see our friends rallying, yet again, to support one of us.

Jared emerged from the back room, and I laughed at how long it had taken him to pull himself together after our kiss. He was grinning as he walked toward me, and I laughed. "You okay there, Cowboy?"

"Oh yes, just needed a minute." He kissed my cheek as he took the stack of chairs from my hands and rolled it into the history section.

I turned and arranged the pair of wingback chairs for Tuck's one-on-ones just behind the self-help shelves. The space would be private for conversation, just like Tuck wanted, but he'd still be in sight of most people so he didn't look like he'd disappeared. As he'd reminded me just a few times, appearances were important.

After I put a small basket with little bottles of water beneath the table between the arms of the two chairs, I added a couple of pillows to both seats and then put two pads of papers and several pens on the table in case Tuck or his constituent wanted to make any notes.

The heart-to-heart space set up, I went to check on Marcus and found him in the middle of a huge red, white, and blue display with a poster-size photo of Tuck front and center on an easel. "You went patriotic?" I said.

"Yeah, not really our favorite, but I figured it was fitting for an election, especially given the way Dooley's crew pulls the God and Country stuff," he said.

I sighed. "Yeah, good point. Thanks. It looks really good."

"Not too much like a funeral?" he asked as he studied Tuck's photograph. "I'm a little worried about this set-up here." He pointed.

"Nah. No flowers here, and from the window, I think it'll have a totally different feel. Go take a look?" I said as I gestured outside.

He jumped off the window platform and out the front door, where he stood studying the display. I took a quick look around the store and found myself grateful, for once, that we didn't have any customers. We could all use a few minutes to just get things set and in place.

"Harvey, got a sec?" Cate called from the café.

"On my way," I said as I gave Marcus a little wave and stepped back into the shop.

It didn't take us long to finish set-up. Cate and Lucas ran through their plan for managing Tuck's time, including a casual five minute warning walk-by with a cute little sign Cate had decorated with sheriff's badges.

Rocky was back and looked more rested after her day off. She had put out a spread of ginger snaps and mints on one of her tables near the café entrance, and I could smell the fresh brewed coffee already.

The chairs were arranged well around the shop, and Jared had put a couple out for Walter and Stephen and Cate and Lucas, too. I started to ask him why he'd put a two chairs out of sight behind the fantasy shelves opposite Tuck's speaking area, but I didn't get a chance because just then Marcus said, "Um, Harvey."

I looked toward the door and found my assistant manager being held with his arms behind his back by Roger Birmingham. "Jared?" I shouted.

He came running from the back of the store and had his gun drawn before he got to me. "Let him go," he said.

"Not until you listen," Birmingham said as he pushed Marcus further into the store. "You need to listen to me, and no one will get hurt."

My heart was racing as I tried to think about what I could do in this moment. If someone came in that door behind Birmingham, I'm not sure what would happen.

"I'm listening," Jared said, "But you don't have to keep a hostage."

"Yes, I do. They're watching," Birmingham said. "Keep your gun up. This needs to look real."

As he and Marcus stepped further into the store, Kara Birmingham came in behind them. "We have your attention now," she shouted as the door closed behind her.

I nodded seriously and tried to slow down my brain as I pieced together what was happening.

"Who is watching?" Cate asked from behind me.

"Dooley and his men. I need for you to hear me out but look like I'm threatening you, okay?"

Jared took a step forward, his gun still drawn and nodded. "Start talking."

Kara Birmingham stepped forward to stand beside her husband. "Dooley killed our daughter. We know it. The proof is in Catherine's apartment, but Dooley is guarding that with his life."

"What kind of proof?" Jared asked.

"Recordings of Dooley threatening her if she left him. Very specific recordings," Roger said.

"You've heard them?" I asked.

Roger nodded. "She played them for us, told us where she was hiding the sim card. She was scared."

"Okay, we can get the recordings, but what is this all about?" I gestured around the store with my arms.

"Dooley wants to be here with his men to before everyone arrives tonight. He wants to 'control the situation,' he said." Roger continued. "He sent us in here to let you know that they are coming in and that if you try to stop them, you will be sorry."

"So how do you want to play this?" Jared said, clearly convinced by Birmingham's statement. "What do we need to know?

"They're all armed," Kara said. "And they won't hesitate to badger and intimidate people if they need to." She put her fingers into the front of her hair and hung her head. "But we don't have a choice."

"Why is that?" I said. "We could all go out the back and call Tuck."

Roger shook his head. "There's a sniper on the roof of the hardware store, and Dooley has Horatio and Hugo over there."

I really wanted to kneel down and look out the window above the stage to see if I could spot the glint off the sniper's scope, like they do in the movies, but I was too dumb-founded with fear and danger to even move. "A sniper?!"

"This is like an action movie," Lucas groaned. "What do we do?"

"We let them do whatever they want," Jared answered as he looked at me. "Trust me?"

I took a deep breath and nodded. "Of course."

"Alright," Jared said as he holstered his gun. "Go deliver the all-clear. We'll stay in sight and let his men come in whenever they're ready."

I studied Birmingham's face, and all I saw there was fear and anger. But not anger at any of us. No, Birmingham had some real rage, but he wasn't the threat here, at least not to anyone in the store at the moment.

Kara turned and walked briskly out the door as Birmingham said in Marcus's ear, "Act like I pushed you to the ground."

Marcus did a very convincing tumble to the floor of the store, and Rocky charged over from the café to check on him, a decision which I figured was part show and part genuine concern.

"Now what?" I said to Jared.

"Believe it or not, Harvey, it's all going according to plan," he leaned over and whispered, "Trust me" and then gave me a quick hug before stepping toward the door and standing near Birmingham, one hand on his gun.

A few moments later, a string of white, mostly middle-aged men came streaming into my shop. I saw a few mostly gray heads, too, and two men who looked to be in their twenties came in last. But it was a certain slightly bushy gray head that caught my attention most: Woody.

I did the very best I could not to let my gaze stay on him too long, and I resisted the urge to glance over at Jared for some kind of confirmation of what I was seeing.

For his part, Woody didn't even look at me. He just walked in, seated himself in a chair by the register, and played his part to a tee.

As the men sat down, Jared said, "Gentlemen, it's good to see you. Now we're not looking for trouble here, okay?"

One of the men who had come in first said, "You don't make trouble, you won't have any deputy."

"Traitor," I heard one of the young men whisper and only then realized that these guys all knew Jared from his day with them undercover. Suddenly, everything felt much more dangerous. These were men with some real anger issues, clearly, and I didn't like that my boyfriend might be a target of their anger.

"Just doing my job, fellows," Jared said and then took a seat by the door.

At that moment, my parents returned with Henri and Bear and big bunches of balloons. "Thought we'd make things look a bit more festive," Mom said as she walked toward the stage and hung two huge groups of red, white, and blue balloons right in front of the window.

"Thanks, Mom," I said as I followed her to help her secure the decorations. "Good idea." I had no clue what was going on, but I did know my mother found balloons to be entirely tacky except at a children's birthday party. So something was up.

The store felt heavy with tension, but we had an event to host and potentially a lot of people on their way in. So with a nod from Jared, we went back to preparing. Mom helped Rocky finish the coffee and put out pitchers of cream and milk while Marcus and I did a final walk-through to tidy the store. Dad and Jared talked quietly by the register, and as customers began to stream in, Stephen and Walter greeted everyone and pointed them to Cate and Lucas if they wanted to sign-up for time with Tuck.

Dad milled around handing out brochures, and Marcus took care of the book-related questions while I staffed the register. The turn-out was good, and while part of me was thrilled because that meant things looked good for Tuck's campaign, I was also far more nervous to have all these people here with the Identity Dixie boys on hand.

Still, Jared said he had it all under control, and I needed to believe he was right. So I did, and I pushed myself the best I could to just act like this was any other night in my bookstore.

12

Tuck and Lu arrived, as planned, right at seven, and after spending fifteen minutes greeting everyone and getting a cup of decaf, he headed to his seat and Cate escorted the young woman who wanted to talk to him to her seat across from him.

Just like that, the event was off, and when Elle and Pickle came in a few minutes late, I was able to greet them and give them a very quick heads up about the situation while we all got coffee. Both of them kept their faces neutral as I explained, and when we went back to the bookstore, they milled and talked with people as if it was the most natural thing in the world.

Tuck was onto his third one-on-one when Mart arrived. She'd been in Baltimore all day for a conference for vineyards, and while both Tuck and I had assured her that she didn't need to travel back for this, she had insisted. Now, I was very glad to see her because I needed her presence. Unfortunately, just as she arrived, Bryan Dooley himself came into the store, and I didn't have a minute to catch Mart up to speed because the tension had ratcheted way up with the other candidate's arrival.

My first thought was to ask him to leave, but given that most of the people in my store had no idea what was going on behind the scenes and that I didn't want to hurt Tuck's campaign by being what appeared to be rude to the other candidate, I smiled and greeted him, inviting him to get some coffee.

Fortunately, all the one-on-one slots with Tuck were taken, so Dooley didn't even have the option to corner Tuck, but unfortunately Tuck was about to take his first break of the evening. I had no doubt that Dooley knew that and had timed his entrance accordingly. He certainly had spies everywhere tonight.

Just as Tuck stood up for his first break, Dooley approached him, and I heard Lu, standing near at the register, groan quietly. "Sheriff Mason, I wonder if you might fancy an impromptu debate?"

Tuck sighed and then nodded. I knew he hated to be put on the spot like this, but I also knew that if he refused, he'd look both afraid and unprepared.

"Mrs. Beckett," Dooley said, "I believe you have some microphones. May we use them?"

"First of all, it's *Ms.* Beckett, and no, you may not. We have a schedule tonight, and there is not room for a debate on it. The people of St. Marin's have signed up for conversations with Sheriff Mason, and as the organizer of this event, I must insist we honor those commitments."

I heard a small murmur of approval pass through the crowd behind me, and I continued. "If, however, you'd like to talk with a few of your potential supporters in one-on-ones, we could definitely accommodate that." I had no idea what I was doing, but this felt right. When I looked at Jared, I felt a little panicky. Maybe this was going to thwart his plan.

But he just looked at me and smiled and nodded. "Good idea," he mouthed.

Dooley appeared to consider that for a second and then said, "Alright then. Anyone want to talk to me?"

I have to give my town's citizens credit – they are kind people, and in this moment, even though people were obviously here to support Tuck, they stepped up and signed up to talk with Dooley. Cate and Lucas created another sign-up sheet, and we offered to stay open an extra hour so that more people could talk to the candidates.

Within a couple of minutes, all of Dooley's spaces and the four extra for Tuck were filled, and Rocky had more coffee on and a new batch of cookies in the oven. She was going to have a good night if the foot traffic into the café aligned with her sales.

The bookstore side of things wasn't doing too bad either. Marcus and I were recommending books left and right, and I even heard my mom put in a good word for Diana Gabaldon. She was obsessed with Outlander, and the pitch she gave to the woman waiting to talk with Tuck created another convert. We sold the first three books in the series to Mom's new friend before she left the store, and I expected that if she, like most of Gabaldon's readers, loved the series, she'd be back in a few days for the rest.

For the rest of the night, I was a bit on edge and worried both about what the Dixie Boys would do but also about how quiet and reserved Woody had been. He wasn't normally a chatterbox by any means, but this distance he was keeping around himself had me nervous. I hoped he was just playing his part, not finding he had to protect himself in some major psychological manner.

At ten, when Tuck and Dooley finished their final one-on-ones, I quickly began to hustle the remaining customers out of the store. I was tired, but I was also anxious to get Dooley's posse out of my store. Fortunately, the two men who had taken the oddly placed seats on the other side of the shelf by Tuck plus two other guys who had been sipping coffee in the café for the entire evening identified themselves when I informed them they were leaving, and so we had six police officers on hand to help us move everyone along.

Once Dooley's men, including Woody, and the customers were gone, my friends made quick work of tidying the store, stacking the chairs, and helping Rocky clean the café. Then, all of us headed out en masse to go home and wind down. From the wan looks on my friends' faces, the night had taken a toll on them, too.

When Jared offered to drive Mart and I home, Mart bowed out, saying she was meeting Symeon at the restaurant and that she'd see us later. She winked at me and then jogged up the street and stepped inside Chez Cuisine.

I had to admit I didn't mind a little alone time with Jared, especially after this day, so when he said he didn't mind putting the pups in the back of the cruiser, we loaded them up and made the short drive home.

Since I knew I needed a little wind down time before bed, I invited Jared in to watch an episode of *Married at First Sight* with me. He was a good sport and even got me a cup of hot tea while I queued up the episode. Then, we spent forty-five minutes making snide comments about the dude who, quite obviously, wasn't at all interested in the woman he had agreed to marry.

When the show ended, I didn't want Jared to leave, and I told him so. "Good," he said, "because I don't want to leave either."

I leaned over and gave him a lingering kiss. "Thank you for today. Thank you for not telling me about Woody and thank you for trusting me to be able to handle it."

"You were remarkable tonight, Harvey Beckett. You're so quick on your feet, and even when things could go horribly wrong, you stay strong and kind. Just two of the reasons I love you."

I smiled, and then his words processed all the way through the synapses in my brain. "You love me?"

"That's what I said," Jared said with a wry smile.

I stared at him for a long minute with my mouth half open, and then I said, "I love you, too."

THE NEXT MORNING, when I came out into the living room, Symeon was snoring away on the couch. I moved as quietly as I could to make coffee and put on bacon and eggs for all of us, but it didn't take long for the smell to wake the three other people in the house.

Fortunately, Mart came out first, so I was able to give her a heads up that Jared had stayed over before he came out of my room in his slightly crumpled uniform. To her credit, she said simple, "Good" and then went over to give her groggy boyfriend a kiss on the couch.

Jared slipped his arms around me while I flipped the bacon. "Good morning, lovely," he whispered in my ear.

"Good morning," I said as I leaned back to kiss him. "You sleep okay?"

"You mean did I sleep well in your rock-hard bed made from the same stone from which they carved Stonehenge?"

I turned and looked at him. "I take it you sleep in a pile of pillows à la the Princess and the Pea?"

"Pillow top, woman. That's all I'm saying. Pillow. Top." Then he kissed me again and went to pour the coffee.

I laughed and plated up the breakfast before carrying two very full platters to the table and then going back for the plate of buttered toast I'd also made. Everyone filled their plates, and the silence of the hungry and tired settled around us.

Eventually, though, Mart said, "Can we talk about our trip this weekend now?"

Jared and Symeon looked at each other and said, in unison, "What trip?"

Mart's eyes grew wide, and she glared at me. "You didn't tell him?"

"You didn't tell *him*?" I said with a tilt of my head toward Symeon.

"Kidding, women," Symeon said. "We're just playing with you."

"Of course, Harvey told me, Mart. I'm looking forward to it," Jared added. "Dwayne Johnson is a hero of mine."

I looked at my boyfriend out of the corner of my eye. "Hero, huh?"

"Okay, muscularly speaking," Jared said, and all of us cracked up.

For the next half-hour, all the worries of the past few days slid away as we planned our road trip snacks, talked about who would control the radio, and made the all-important decision about whose car we were taking. Well, that wasn't really a decision because Symeon had just bought the new Tesla SUV, so it was really a no-brainer there.

Eventually, though, our conversation circled back around to the night before. Mart had given Symeon the full run-down, and while he'd said he was glad to miss it, he also said he wished Mart had called him. "I don't like that you were there without your person," he said.

"Oh, you're my person now, huh?" she said.

"Am I not?" Symeon said. "Does Harvey still take that title?"

"Nope, it's you, mister," she said and kissed him.

I rolled my eyes and said, "You two could have your own CW show?"

Jared laughed. "Honestly, we are a sort of middle-aged CW, aren't we? All we're missing is a love triangle."

"And a werewolf," Mart added.

"Dibs on the werewolf," Symeon said as he stood up and got Mart's coat. "Drive you to work?"

"You picking me up later?" she asked.

"Of course," he said as he walked with her to the door. "Thanks for breakfast, Harvey."

"Have a good day you two," I said as I cleared the rest of the table. "Give us a lift too?"

"Of course," Jared said as he got my coat. "I can't be shown up now can I?"

"I think last night established – in many ways – that no one can show you up, sir," I said as I kissed him on the cheek. "Thank you for staying."

"Tonight, my place?" he asked.

I stared at him and said, "So we're doing this then? For real?"

"As real as it gets, Ms. Beckett. I even bought dog beds for just such an occasion." He leashed up the dogs and headed for the door. "Pick you up here at six? I'll have dinner ready."

"Perfect," I said. That would give me just enough time to pack an overnight bag after work. "Now, Jeeves, to All Booked Up."

"Yes, m'lady," he said with a bow.

WITH TWO BIG and successful events under our belts in just a few days, I was riding pretty high when I opened up the store that morning. Rocky was also looking pretty chipper as she whistled her way through her own opening routine.

"Good night last night?" I asked when I went over to get my latte.

"Great night in sales and just a good night in general," she said. "Given that the deputy was not as freshly pressed as usual I take it you had a good night, too." She gave me a lingering wink.

"Great night . . . which was so lovely after all the shenanigans here. Did you see Woody at all?"

"You mean the nearly catatonic man in the corner? Yeah, I saw him. It was creepy."

"Wasn't it?!" I shook my head. "I hope he's okay. Jared said he's undercover for one more day just to see what he can figure out about Catherine Birmingham."

"Yeah, what was all that with her parents last night? They hung around all evening, probably because they had to, but then they just left with Dooley like it was nothing."

I had noticed that, too, but given that we weren't supposed to know the Birminghams had tipped us off, I didn't point it out when they were leaving. They were undercover in some kind of way, too. "It's all weird, and Jared doesn't quite know what to make of them either. He believes what they said about Dooley and their daughter, but why they are working with him at all is a total mystery."

Rocky shook her head. "Grief does weird things to people, I guess." She looked down at my almost empty mug. "Need an immediate refill?"

"Oh yes, please," I said.

The day went by without incident. We sold a lot of books. Galen and Mack came in a day late for their Tuesday shopping trip, having missed yesterday for an appointment. I had five lattes because I was so sleep-deprived. And by the time five o'clock rolled around, I knew I was either going to fly home or fall asleep as soon as I got there. So I took another latte for the walk.

It was starting to get dark just after five, but I didn't think much about it. The streets were well-lit, and the walk was short. Still, when I turned up Main that night, I got a chill up the back of my neck. Something felt off.

I kept the dogs' leashes a bit tighter than usual, and I wasn't sure whether to feel relieved or more frightened when they seemed completely relaxed and at ease. Still, we made it home just fine, and when I double-checked that everything was locked up tight before heading to my bedroom to pack my bag, I felt myself relax. Just a little.

Not enough though because when Jared rang the bell thirty minutes later, I almost jumped out of my skin. I had decided to get in a few more chapters of my book while I waited, and I was deep into a great scene when he rang.

My breath was still short when I opened the door to him a few seconds later. "You ready?" he said, and then he saw my face. "What's wrong?"

I shook my head. "Nothing. I just got a little weirded out for some reason on the walk home, and then the doorbell startled me. I'm fine." I bent over and picked up my bag and then called the dogs.

As Jared put on their leashes, he said, "None of you have to worry. We'll all be together tonight." His tone was light, but I caught him looking up at me with concern.

I decided to try to play off my continued edginess with humor. "So what are you feeding me, sir?"

"Grilled cheese and tomato soup," he said simply.

"Are you serious?" I asked.

He looked down at me as he prepared to close my door on his car. "Yes, why?"

I smiled. "Because I can't think of something that would taste better tonight. Perfecto," I gave my fingers a kiss.

"And you don't even know about the three kinds of cheese and the basil yet," he said as he sat down next to me. "You're beautifully simple."

"That's one of the kindest things anyone has ever said to me. Thank you."

As we climbed out of the car at his house a couple of minutes later, he said, "All I have to do is cook everything. All the prep is done, so come in, have a glass of wine, and tell me about your day."

I liked the sound of that, but I didn't like the next sound I heard. A scuffle and a hard grunt from the other side of the car followed by the frantic barking of the dogs.

It was completely dark, so even at this short distance I couldn't see much in the light from Jared's porch. But I did see my boyfriend struggling against what looked to be two, maybe three men.

"Get inside, Harvey," Jared shouted. "Take the dogs."

The authority in his voice made me move without hesitation, and I flung open the car door and watched as two huge animals lunged past me toward Jared.

Shouts followed, and then one of the men said, "Call them off or I'll put them down."

I still couldn't see what the situation was with Jared, but I knew he wouldn't want the dogs to be killed, not if he could help it. So I called them back to me, and for once, they listened and came. They continued to growl, but when I started to move toward Jared's house, they flanked me, backing up just like I did until we were at the porch.

That's when I heard him behind me. "Ms. Beckett, what a surprise. We weren't expecting to see you tonight."

I turned around to see Bryan Dooley leaning against the frame of Jared's front door. The dogs let out a volley of barks that made me wince, but then they spun on their heels and took off down the road.

Dooley laughed. "Some guard dogs there," he said.

I didn't dare turn my head to watch the hounds run, but I knew my dogs. They weren't running away. Dooley didn't need to know that though. "Some things are just too scary for the most brave among us," I said.

Jared snorted behind me, and I marveled not only at my ability to be witty and cutting in this situation but also at Jared's laughter. Then, I remembered he was more accustomed to this kind of thing than I was and smiled. If he was laughing, I suspected he had a plan. Just that thought calmed me enough to make me braver, too.

I marched up the steps to Jared's house and turned my back toward where Jared and his captors were still shrouded in darkness. "You coming or what?" I looked back at Dooley. "I imagine this is a kidnapping situation, am I right?"

Dooley glared at me. "Bring him inside," he spat and then grabbed my arm and almost pulled me off my feet backwards.

Before I slipped through the doors, I had just enough of a view of Jared and the men around him in the porch light to see that Woody and Roger Birmingham were two of the three. Jared winked at me just as I was tugged beyond the door and shoved into Jared's living room.

Jared tumbled in soon after me, and I heard the front door slam shut. I looked over at Jared, and he shook his head slightly before putting a finger to his lips. He didn't want us to give anything away, and I imagined he was especially eager to hide the fact that Dooley and his one true ally were outnumbered, four to two.

I nodded and let my head fall back to the floor. If we were going to be held captive, even sort of, I figured I might as well grab a few minutes of rest.

Jared slid over next to me, laid out on his back, too, then slid his hand over mine. I stifled a giggle as I realized we were in some sort of strange Savasana. I didn't think most yogis had the chance to surrender to the earth in the midst of their own kidnapping, but I decided to give it a go and let out a long, slow breath.

In the hallway, I could hear the low rumble of the men's voices, but I couldn't make out what they were saying. I wasn't sure exactly why Woody and Birmingham were still going along with whatever plan of Dooley's this was, but I figured there had to be a reason. At least I wanted to think that, so I tamped down the rising fear that maybe Birmingham wasn't really on our side and that maybe, just maybe, Woody had been swayed somehow to think Dooley was in the right.

My logical mind knew that idea was ridiculous – Woody was one of the most loving and generous men, I knew, and he adored Tuck. The Identity Dixie ideals were just not his. But even in Savasana with the man I loved beside me, I couldn't quite keep my fear tamped down.

After a few moments, the men walked into the room, and Dooley laughed. "Catching a nap?"

"I'll take them where I can get them," I said as I sat up, folded my hands, and formally closed my yoga practice. "Now, what is going on?" I stood up and walked calmly to Jared's couch before sitting down.

Jared sat up but didn't move from his spot on the floor. Dooley blocked the door to the hallway, and Birmingham and Woody moved into the room with Woody taking a seat next to me on the couch.

"Well, our friend Deputy Watson here is a traitor, and we don't think too kindly of traitors," Dooley said. "Do we boys?"

Both Woody and Birmingham shook their heads vigorously, and I felt my nerves grow taut. All the fears I'd had about my friend and this man who had seemed so sincere rose to the surface.

It didn't help that they quickly and efficiently found ropes in Jared's basement and tied us to two of his dining room chairs by our wrists and ankles. I kept watching Woody's face, hoping I'd see a wink or a long gaze to reassure me, but he was stern or laughing at Dooley's supposed jokes.

I tried to keep calm by taking deep breaths and trusting what I knew of my friend Woody and the competent able police man I knew Jared to be, but when the henchmen I didn't know came back up from Jared's basement a second time with a nail gun, the sweat started to pour out of me. I looked to Jared for reassurance, but his brave face had faded as fast as my bravado. This was bad.

As the man stood with the nail gun hanging casually by his side, Dooley turned to Birmingham and said, "You're sure the sheriff is convinced of those two hardware idiots' guilt?"

Birmingham nodded. "Absolutely certain. He bought what Kara and I said hook, line, and sinker. I expect he'll be making arrests this evening, actually." He looked at his watch.

"I think so too," Woody said. "Heard him talking to her last night." He tilted his head my way. "Seems like he's only struggling with how much he likes those murderers."

I stared at Woody for a long moment and then looked over at Jared. I could see just the bit of a smile at the corner of his lips, but he shoved it away quickly. Tuck had told me no such thing last night, and Woody knew it. So did Jared. I felt a flush of relief wash from the tip of my fingers all the way to my scalp. That was our signal.

For a brief minute I pondered the trick I'd seen in movies where people fall over violently to break the legs and arms off the chair and get free, but these chairs were well-made. With my luck, the only arm I'd break would be my own. I'd just have to wait for Woody to make his move.

Fortunately, the wait wasn't long. Dooley made some impassioned speech about the true identity of America, a diatribe full of historical inaccuracies, prejudice so deep it felt innate, I'm sure, and misogyny so ugly that I wanted to bite the man's nose off. But aside from feeling rage rising inside of me, I largely ignored what he said because I wanted to be sure I was ready for whatever happened next.

Then, just as it appeared Dooley was going to give his guy the order to kill us, Woody said, "Let me do it, Doo. I'll make it look just like what you did to that girl, fix it all up real good for those brothers. Seal the deal."

Dooley stared at him a moment and then said, "Okay. Just two nails." He then pointed to two spots on Jared's head. "Here and here."

Woody took the nail gun from the other man, and at that moment, the front door slammed open and Mayhem and Taco led a bustle of people into the living room while at the same moment, Tuck shouted, "Police" from the back door.

Everyone poured into the living room just as Woody turned the nail gun toward Dooley and Birmingham tackled the other man.

Jared and I looked at each other, and then we began to laugh.

13

W ithin minutes, they were handcuffed and being led out the door while Jared and I were freed and escorted to the couch, where Elle handed us tea that she'd made in Jared's kitchen.

As we sipped, Woody lifted his shirt and detached the thin microphone from just below his collar bone, and then Birmingham followed suit. Both men handed Tuck the wires and then collapsed into the other two chairs across from us. Suddenly, I felt like an idiot for having any doubts. They both looked exhausted and more relieved than I'd ever seen anyone look in my life.

"Sorry I couldn't give you more to reassure you, Harvey," Woody said after Elle had given him his own tea. "Dooley's a sly one, and I couldn't risk it."

I nodded. "I was worried for a bit. I'm sorry. I shouldn't have been."

Woody waved a hand through the air. "It's actually kind of a compliment. Maybe I should have gone into theater." He smiled at me and then let his head fall back against the chair.

"Thank you," Birmingham said to Woody. "Truly. You were the one who got the confession."

Woody shook his head. "If it was my girl, I'd have wanted help, too. Thanks for letting me."

Birmingham sighed. "I hope I never have to return the favor."

I looked from Jared to Woody and then back. Now wasn't the time, but it sure did sound like Woody was saying he had a daughter. I didn't know anything about that, and somehow that was the most surprising thing about the whole night.

DOOLEY and his men were arraigned the next day. Dooley was charged with murder, kidnapping, and threat of death against Tuck. Most of the other members of Identity Dixie were charged with accessory to murder and kidnapping, thanks to Woody and Roger Birmingham's excellent undercover work. They'd been able to capture enough conversation on their recordings to not only provide evidence of the crimes committed but also supply a motive.

"So Dooley had an affair with Catherine?" I asked Woody the next night when all of us gathered at the bookstore for a potluck dinner in Woody's honor.

"Yep, it was brief but quite intense apparently. But then he found out she had an addiction problem, and suddenly she wasn't going to be the perfect 'arm candy' and became a liability instead," Woody said.

Tuck added, "He tried to get her to disappear, but she was trying hard to get herself together. In fact, the reason she was back was that she wanted to make amends. That's why she came to see Horatio and Hugo. She hoped they would help her find a rehab center and then get herself settled here in town while she worked for them to try and pay them back for what she'd stolen. Now that she's gone, the Birminghams have promised to make it right."

Cate groaned. "But Dooley thought she was telling them about her affair with him, and he got scared."

"Exactly," Jared said. "It was terrible, and Kara and Roger are going to get some real help with the anger they feel. But I think they'll make it."

"So what is the story with them? Were they actually her legal foster parents?" Rocky asked. "What was all that about no records?

"That was a mistake on my part, I'm sorry to say. The records for her relinquishment into the foster system had gotten destroyed in a fire we had here at the juvenile court about ten years ago. I should have thought of that, but I was too busy looking for suspects." Tuck hung his head.

Lu hugged her husband and said, "You made a mistake in judgment, sure, but you didn't act on it because you didn't have any real evidence. That's why you're such a good sheriff. You wait for proof."

Stephen raised his glass of bourbon and toasted Tuck, who was certainly a shoe-in for sheriff now that his only competition was in jail and had been exposed as a verifiable white supremacist. Some of the people in our town weren't always very open to people they considered different, but they weren't dumb enough to put their vote behind someone who made their lives off of hate. At least that's what I was choosing to believe.

THAT FRIDAY, bright and early, Mart, Symeon, Jared, and I got into Symeon's new car and drove west into Virginia. As we pulled into the foothills, the colors of autumn came into full brilliance, and every time we passed a sugar maple with its orange and gold glow, I pointed it out to everyone.

By the time we were near The Rock's farm, the common refrain had become, "Look a sugar maple." Except instead of actually pointing out sugar maples, my friends used the phrase to note the barest, scrawniest trees out there. Clearly, the space for my enthusiasm for autumn had closed.

As we turned onto his driveway, Mart said, "Two rules, okay? One: Have fun. Two: No murders."

"Agreed," I said as I took Jared's hand. "I'll do my best."

Jared kissed my cheek. "That's what I'm afraid of," he said.

HARVEY AND MARCUS'S BOOK RECOMMENDATIONS

Here, you will find all the books that Harvey and Marcus recommend in *Epilogue To An Epitaph*. Don't pile them too high on your nightstand. :)

- *A Spindle Splintered* by Alix E. Harrow
- *Change Sings* by Amanda Gorman
- *The Library of the Dead* by T. L. Huchu
- *Hard Landing* by Stephen Leather
- *The Ten Thousand Doors of January* by Alix E. Harrow
- *Murder in the Mystery Suite* by Ellery Adams
- *Once And Future Witches* by Alix E. Harrow
- *Practical Magic* by Alice Hoffman
- *The Hazel Wood* by Melissa Albert
- *The Black Prism* by Brent Weeks
- *The Last Wish* by Andrzej Sapkowski
- *Garden Spells* by Sarah Addison Allen
- *Where The Wild Things Are* by Maurice Sendak
- *The Most Beautiful Thing* by Koa Kalia Young
- *Sulwe* by Lupita Nyong'o
- *The Boy With Big, Big Feelings* by Briney Winn Lee

- *Body in the Attic* by Judi Lynn
- *The Moonlight Child* by Karen McQuestion
- *Remains of the Day* by Kazuo Ishiguro
- *Eragon* by Christopher Paolini
- *Dragonsong* by Anne McCaffrey
- *Vanilla Bean Vampire* by Selina J. Eckert
- *A Psalm for the Wild-Built* by Becky Chambers
- *The Mermaid's Child* by Jo Baker
- *The Mezzanine* by Nicholson Baker
- *Tristran Strong Destroys The World* by Kwame Mbala
- *The Little Prince* by Antoine S. Expert
- *His Dark Materials* by Philip Pullman

I have read all of these books and enjoyed them all for various reasons. I hope you may as well.

Happy Reading!

— ACF

WANT TO READ ABOUT HARVEY'S FIRST SLEUTHING EXPEDITION?

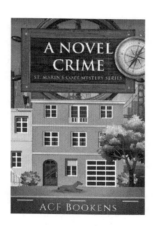

Join my Cozy Up email group for weekly book recs & a FREE copy of *A Novel Crime*, the prequel to the St. Marin's Cozy Mystery Series.
Sign-up here - https://bookens.andilit.com/CozyUp

ABOUT THE AUTHOR

ACF Bookens lives in the Southwest Mountains of Virginia, where the mountain tops remind her that life is a rugged beauty of a beast worthy of our attention. When she's not writing, she enjoys chasing her son around the house with the full awareness she will never catch him, cross-stitching while she binge-watches police procedurals, and reading everything she can get her hands on. Find her at acfbookens.com

    f facebook.com/BookensCozyMysteries
    BB bookbub.com/authors/acfbookens

ALSO BY ACF BOOKENS

St. Marin's Cozy Mystery Series

Publishable By Death

Entitled To Kill

Bound To Execute

Plotted For Murder

Tome To Tomb

Scripted To Slay

Proof Of Death

Epilogue of An Epitaph

Hardcover Homicide

Stitches In Crime Series

Crossed By Death

Bobbins and Bodies

Hanged By A Thread

Counted Corpse

Stitch X For Murder

Sewn At The Crime - Coming in January 2022

Blood And Backstitches - Coming in March 2022

Fatal Floss - Coming April 2022

Strangled Skein - Coming in May 2022

~

Poe Baxter Books Series

Fatalities And Folios - Coming in July 2022

Butchery And Bindings - Coming in September 2022

Massacre And Margins - Coming in October 2022